about 35,000
words

bradleybleckwehl@gmail.com

. / SUPERNATURAL SEX COLLECTION 1 / 2

SUPERNATURAL SEX COLLECTION 1

by
Bradley Bleckwehl

DEMON BABY DADDY 1 – DEVIL SEED

Brooke stepped out of the shower she'd just had as part of her preparation for her big meeting. You see, she'd been lucky enough to get a face to face scheduled with one of the richest men in the country.. billionaire Lucas Morningstar, who would hopefully fund her next expedition in search of an ancient artifact that was said to have the power to give eternal youth. Between that ancient tale and the rumors about Lucas being an actual demon, she didn't know what to take as truth. What she did know though, was that finding that artifact could not only make her famous and rich, highly successful in her field as well as maybe giving her eternal youth, but also that Lucas, demon or not, was consistently placed at the top of eligible rich bachelor lists and he had a ferocious sexual appetite. While in the shower, after shaving herself nice and neat, she'd thought deep on what Lucas might ask of her or do to her in exchange for the funding and the thought of his sexy billionaire self bending her over his desk, pressing her face against it as he pounded away at her pussy to get his rocks off had her rubbing one out in the shower, giving her clit a steamy, soapy rubbing that made her so weak at the knees she fell to sitting down before she could finish herself off. An hour later, she made it to his penthouse apartment from the hotel she was staying at. His assistant, a gorgeous young woman in red, barely out of college age, or maybe not, had Brooke wait while Lucas finished up another meeting in a different room. There was shouting heard from back there before a different man came stumbling out fast with a look of fear on his face. The assistant opened the elevator door for him to get out in and gave him a smack on the ass o his way out. As the elevator doors were closing, Lucas strode calmly but confidently out into the main area, dressed all in black. "Don't ever do business with angels. You can't trust anyone who doesn't have at least a little dirt on their wings."

Brooke moved towards him to meet him with her hand held out to greet. "Mr Morningstar, I'm Brooke.."

He took her hand in his, quickly clasping his other around it too. "The seeker of eternal youth and other mystical artifacts. How exciting a life you must lead. I bet you're wings get dirty from time to time, don't they."

Brooke gave a wink. "Oh it can get real dirty out there. But that's how the goodies are found."

Lucas put an arm around Brooke and said to her as he led her towards the bar. "When you get as rich as I am, there's only certain types of goodies that spark interest. Let's have a drink and discuss the goodies you're seeking and how I can benefit."

They reached the bar where Lucas went to pour them drinks, but Brooke stopped him, tapped at a different bottle. Impressed, he nodded and poured drinks from that one instead. "Good eye, great taste you have."

She drank from her glass, licking her lips seductively after she did. "You don't even know yet."

Grinning, Lucas replied. "Oh you are a devilish one, aren't you? I wager there's not much you wouldn't do to achieve your goals."

Brooke gave a playful shrug as she drank some more of her drink. "Everything in this world has a price. We're a part of this world, aren't we."

It was Lucas' turn to shrug. "Well, you are. Me… not so much, but we'll get to that soon before we discuss my terms for funding your wonderful adventure."

Brooke could swear she saw a flicker of red flare up in Lucas' eyes which frightened her, just a little though. It also got her heart beating quicker as she leant over the bar to expose her cleavage more while tracing her finger around the inner edge of his drink before sucking her finger clean in her mouth. "I know someone as wealthy as you doesn't need the money, so that could rule out you wanting a percentage of the company I build around the youth artifact. Plus you constantly have your way with models from all parts of this world who thirst to be yours, so giving you myself might not be what you're after. This leaves me intrigued, Lucas."

He grinned. "An intrigued mind is worth more than a thousand closed. Patience, dear. You'll find out soon enough."

His hand brushed a strand of hair from her face. "For now, let's just enjoy these drinks and the views of each other. Then we can get down to the dirty details."

Brooke wondered if he was even going to try and fuck her or not. It disappointed her a little to think he might not, yet the flirting gave her hope. She couldn't help but glance down at his crotch and imagine what his cock looked like. He lived with that big dick energy, and in the true way where he could back it up, not in some arrogant poser way. It excited her when she caught him glance at her breasts and she wondered how hard he'd been trying not to, so to keep the power hand in the situation. She guessed it was kind of redundant when she'd already been glancing at the thick outline in his pants, which would have been rather clear to him to see her doing. As if reading her mind, he leant over the bar, his cock outline resting on the lower bench of it and whispered to her. "Ten inches, but it can adjust to suit its surroundings."

He leant back with a wink as his hand traced over hers which sent tingles down to her pussy. She wasn't sure what he meant by it could adjust to suit its surroundings, I mean, she knew he was hinting at size of cock for different pussies but how? Could he control how erect he got? She couldn't help but look down at it again as he ran a finger up her soft, smooth arm, giving her a sensation like static electricity but instead it was warmth. He gazed into her eyes with a powerful energy that had her eyes locked into his. He said. "I can have pretty much anything I want in this world, no matter what the big guy upstairs thinks about it, but there's one thing I can't just make happen.. well I haven't had the opportunity to maker happen yet. You see, it's just genetics that males want to breed legacy into the world, and even a being such as I isn't immune to that powerful desire. But unlike mortal men, I must be rather picky with who I choose to birth my progeny. "There are plenty of women with fine genetics, exquisite physical genes, wonderful open minds and clever brains and I must say, you do possess all these fine qualities yourself, but alas, there must be deeper ingredients in the mix."

Brooke was taken by surprise. He wanted to impregnate her, for her to carry and give birth to his child, most likely preferring a son. She tried to wrap her mind around it, wondering if that was something she would do to secure what she needed to chase her dreams, or was it a line too far. He studied her as she wracked her brain, waiting for her to say something, which she did. "So… what other qualities do you seek in your potential baby momma?"

He sipped at his drink. "Well.. someone with spirit, heart, courage. They're all wonderful traits I would like my son to have, or daughter. It might actually be more fun having a female progeny take over the world, not having all that toxic testosterone clouding mind and strategy."

Brooke liked the sound of that.. having a daughter be so successful in the world, busting the patriarchy of mortal man. She touched Lucas' arm, ran hand up it and stroked his cheek. "And you've got me in that ideal profile of yours?"

He nodded. She smiled. "That's sweet of you. I'm flattered. So if this was something I agreed to, would it be right away or after my expedition? Because where I'll be going isn't exactly a safe journey for an unborn baby and it could take a long time."

Lucas kissed her hand. "With my seed growing in you, there's really not much in this world that could cause harm to you or the child. I'd be watching over too, of course."

"You'd be coming on the expedition with me?"

Lucas gave a gentle shake of head. "That wasn't what I said, my dear. And by the way, if you're worried about the journey being harder while pregnant, think of how much quicker it'll get done with however much finance you need for it. Think helicopters, professional diving crews, private boats and planes, the best native guides available."

Brooke did think on it before she moved around to the same side of the bar as Lucas to grab a different bottle to pour her next drink. As she reached past him, she grazed her hand against his cock with slow, purposeful touch. "If I'm going to be carrying life inside me soon, I might as well get a taste of the finest drink have here."

He held her with hand on hip as she leant over to grab the bottle. "I like the way you think, queen. Get some desire and danger in before duty."

Brooke stood up in front of Lucas, rubbing her ass against his cock as she did. She stood in front of him with her behind pressed against his dick outline and his hands on her hips as she poured them a new drink each. Feeling his cock growing hard against her, she leant back against him with her face turned to be resting against his, her mouth so close to his as if she was going to kiss him, but then held his drink up to his mouth. "Is this the danger part?"

Lucas took the drink in one hand and used the other to wrap around Brooke's waist. A spark ignited in the energy between them with their bodies so close, it didn't even scare her when his eyes became full glowing red with crackles of lightning through them. He said. "No, but it's close. You think you can handle it?"

Enchanted by the sight of his eyes, she grinded her ass against his cock some more while taking a mouthful of her drink. "Only one way to find out."

He grinned as he enjoyed the feel of her ass working his cock. "You play like you can handle the rough."

She turned around, her lips almost upon his, her hand stroking along his cock. "How rough do you want to get?"

He kissed her for a moment before biting her lip and saying. "Just a bit rougher than you can handle."

She kissed him back. "Let's test some limits then."

She took his nuts in her hand and gave them a squeeze that would have made any mortal man cry out, yet Lucas merely winced a little. "Sweet queen, the only limits getting tested here today will be yours. Last chance to be able to walk away."

She took him by the hand, led him towards the bedroom. "Show me what you've got then, devilish one."

They entered the bedroom where Brooke closed the door. "Your assistant can listen, but what happens next is only for our eyes."

Lucas gave an elbow nudge to a panel in the wall that opened up a hidden section behind it that held numerous BDSM equipment and toys. Brooke came over to admire the selection, trailing her hand across it before selecting a leather whip. She handed it to Lucas and kissed him, bit at his lip. His grin turned into a fierce look as she ordered her with commanding tone. "Get those pants off and get on your knees!"

Already feeling aroused by this, Brooke did as she was told, seductively biting at her own lip as she slid her pants and panties off, tossed the panties at Lucas and got down on her knees, her pussy and ass pointed up at Lucas. "You like the view daddy? You want.."

The whip cracked through the air, punished the tender flesh of Brooke's behind with a strike that made her shriek out in pained shock. Her ass stung, yet despite the pain, her pussy wettened up. Lucas asked her. "Are you still daddy's bad girl or do you need to go home?"

"Yes daddy, I'm your bad g.."

The whip lashed her soft buttcheeks again, causing welts on her ass as she buckled forward a little, cried out in pain. "Argh, I'm your bad girl."

Lucas grabbed a paddle from the wall and got real close to Brooke, rubbed his hand over her bright red ass, slid hand under her and played with her clit. "You need to be punished then!"

As he flicked her clit, he brought the paddle down upon her ass with a solid whack that lurched her forward a little and caused her to howl out, ass roaring raw. Lucas could feel the warmth and wetness of her pussy increasing against his hand as he raised the paddle to strike again. "How bad have you been?"

"Ohhh, I've been terrible, daddy. I've done.."

Whack! The paddle smacked against her ass again, causing a numb feeling that overpowered the pain somewhat. She wondered what would come next as she knelt there on hands and knees, tears welling in her eyes, pussy pulsating heat. She felt his hand move up from her pussy to under her top where he pinched one of her nipples. "You haven't learnt your lesson yet, you naughty bitch! You need more punishment, now get that ass raised higher! NOW!"

Brooke quickly, but tenderly thrust her throbbing red ass up as high as she could get it and winced, waiting for the next hit of pain. "Yes daddy."

Lucas slapped her ass cheeks a few times, as he slid a couple of fingers inside of her before pulling them out and sucking on them. Brooke felt one of his hands grab her on the back of her neck, pushed her head down right before he slid his cock between her hot pussy lips, pushing his knob past them and into her glowing fuckhole along with most of his dick. Brooke yelped from the unexpected entry, so glad to be getting the dick instead of more punishment to her ass. Lucas grabbed a handful of Brooke's hair and jerked her head backwards, turned it to look around at him. "Are you fucking ready for this?!"

"Yes daddy, I'm.."

He scrunched her hair up tight in his fist. "I don't care!"

With her head still controlled by his grip, he started pumping his hips back and forth with wicked aggression, driving her body forward with every follow through of his cock into her, almost making her lose her grip. He seen she was unstable and fucked her even harder which knocked one of her hands out from underneath her, would have caused her to faceplant into the floor if he wasn't yanking her head backwards still. She cried out. "Ohhh fuck, yes daddy. Oh god!"

Upon hearing the lord's name, Lucas smacked Brooke's ass again right where the worst welts were from the previous punishment. "Call me your demon daddy!"

Tears in her eyes from the pain and pleasure, she wailed as her pussy pulsated. "Yes demon daddy, yes! Break my fucking hips demon daddy!"

He let go of her hair and wrapped his hand around her throat. "I'll break what I want, you bad bitch! And you'll cum when I tell you to cum, if I decide to let you!"

She found it hard to breathe with his hand tight on her throat, even more so with his vicious pounding of her pussy that had her yelping and moaning with what breath she could muster. "Oh fuck! Oh demon daddy, please let me cum. I'm going to cum."

He pulled his dick out of her pussy and started slapping it against her raw, beaten ass, bringing cries from her. He spat on her ass crack. "You'll cum when I say you can cum, or I'll shove this dick so far up your ass!"

"Yes, daddy, whatever you say demon daddy."

The feeling of him shoving his devilish dick back into her pussy had her groaning with relief, not caring that she could barely breath, the whole situation having her sopping wet. She could swear it felt like his dick grew bigger inside of her, stretched out against pussy walls to make up for the wetness. It had her on the brink of cuming all over his dick and took all of her willpower not to burst right then, As if sensing it, feeling Brooke's pussy twitching around his cock, he reached around and started flicking her clit too while fucking her hard and said. "Don't you dare fucking cum! Don't even fucking think about it!"

She had to bite down on her own lip to distract from the waves of pleasure building up inside her that had her about to orgasm when all of a sudden she felt his thrusting stop and a oud roar escape him before hot cum started shooting out of his cock and into her pussy. In the midst of his primal groaning, he managed to get the words out. "Now.. now you can cum."

His last few pumps to soothe the remaining demon seed out of cock sent her over the edge too, had her collapse with face on arm on floor as body shook violently while she pushed her pussy back against him to stroke out every last ounce of pleasure she could get from those moments. His hot cum felt so nice filling her up as her pussy squeezed on him, milking the pleasure for all she could before she collapsed, completely exhausted. He pulled out, lifted her up in his arms, carried her to the bed while listening closely to her womb. "Mission accomplished, queen. We both get what we want."

THE END

SCARED STIFF 1 – FUCK ME DEAD

Jess was making the long drive home at night after spending the weekend with family at her parent's home. It was a ten hour drive one way and by the time she'd gotten halfway home, rain was pouring down, making visibility minimal. Desperately wanting to get home to her own warm bed that night, she tried driving on at a slower pace, the rain beating against the windscreen, wipers failing to keep up with the downpour. She leant forward and drove slower to try to gain better sight squinting to see anything when lights appeared right in front of her and a loud horn blared from a truck speeding past the other way, smashed off her side mirror as it continued on away. "Shit!"

She hadn't even realized she'd been creeping over to the wrong side of the road. Heart raced as she pulled off to the side, a panicked sweat built up despite the cold, heart trying to thump out of her chest. It was only when she was barely moving at all that she could start to make out her position on the road and was finally able to find a 'safe' spot to park off it. The rain eased off after about another hour, yet that hour dragged on as there was no phone service out there and Jess had to fight off sleep as she really didn't want to be sitting out there asleep and alone, so vulnerable. When the rain finally did ease off enough for her to feel safe driving again, she found she couldn't get the car moving, could only spin the tires in the muddy ground under her. Despite ten minutes of trying, she only managed to make things worse by churning up the soaked ground even more. The inability to move and the lack of phone service had her out of the car, walking around to try to find some service or a nearby home she could use the phone of. No matter how much she walked around, she only managed to collect more mess on shoes than any actual phone service. Mood got worse and worse as the rain started pouring down again when she was pretty far from her car. A faint light in the distance gave her hope as she seen the beginning of a driveway. The monstrous cracking of thunder right above her head had her moving as fast as she could down the messy driveway to try to reach what was hopefully a home. Huge relief was felt as she found a house with lights on. Almost rudely with nerves she banged at the door to be heard over the pouring of rain and clapping of thunder. No footsteps were heard which gave her a fright when the door swung open to reveal a tall, bearded, decent looking guy there. Jess said. 'Hey, I'm so sorry to disturb you, my car broke down and it's.."

He waved her in with warm smile. "Come in, come in, you must be freezing, you're soaked."

Now normally there'd be no way she'd enter some strange guys home, especially out in the middle of nowhere, but the situation was dire and his smile and tone of voice carried such friendly, non-threatening warmth. She eagerly obliged entering the home to escape the wet and the cold, kicking off her muddy shoes at the doorway as she did. The guy guided her inside with one hand as the door slammed shut by itself behind them. Jess jumped from that noise, pulled away from the guy who looked shocked too as he said. "Damn! That wind almost brought on a heart attack, haha. I can't imagine how it must have been for you out there. I'm Paul by the way."

He grabbed a blanket from the nearby couch and offered it to Jess as well as his hand to shake. She gratefully accepted the blanket to wrap around herself to warm up, dry off, then accepted the handshake. It felt nice, warm, welcoming, and the smile he gave with it gave her extra warmth inside, caused the holding of hands to linger. He was the first to let go, although his fingers traced softly over her skin as he did, sending excited chills through her, causing a different type of warmth inside. "Nice to meet you, Paul. I'm Jess."

His smile beamed brighter. "Nicer to meet you Jess. I'm glad I can be of help."

She started to feel even safer. Faint footsteps creaked the floorboards above in the second floor of the house. "Is that your wife? Or kid?"

Paul chuckled, shook his head. "No, no, I'm single, no kids. That's just my cat. He thinks he owns the second floor, haha."

"Awww that's pretty cute."

Despite the being inside and the blanket, Jess shivered, which Paul noticed. "Would you like something hot to eat, I can throw some leftovers in the microwave for you."

Jess was actually hungry and liked the sound of some warm food to heat her up more. She'd thought the blanket and being inside would be enough but she couldn't shake the cold chills that kept touching upon her. "I don't want to be anymore of a bother than needed. Do you have any service on your phone or a landline I could use though? I need to call a towing service."

Paul keenly pulled his phone from his pocket. "Of course, no problem."

He tapped to unlock it before handing it to Jess who quickly saw it had no service either. "Argh, no service on yours either."

He took it back, glanced at it. "Ah, damn, This bloody storm. Clouds and rain always mess with the reception out here. I'm sorry."

The sincere look of feeling bad in Paul from not being able to help Jess that way had her feel for him. She touched his arm, gave it a caring rub. "It's all good. What leftovers have you got we can heat up?"

Before too long they were sitting on the small couch together, finishing off some hot food and watching a dvd. It nice, comfy. Even without intent, their legs rested against each other tanks to the small size of the couch, yet before too long, their bodies drew closer to each other instead of resting against the sides of the couch. Thunder struck again, rattling the roof of the home, shaking the windows which had Jess pulling up even closer to Paul who instinctively wrapped an arm around her to help her feel safe. His arm around her felt strong, but safe, comforting so she nestled into it, took his other hand in hers. Icey breath appeared from the darkness of an a joining room behind them as light reflected in a pair of eyes behind the breath. An intimate scene of physical romance played on the dvd Jess and Paul were watching which got her feeling a certain type of way. It seemed it had Paul feeling the same as he moved her hand from his thigh to the bulge of his cock in his pants. With her hand admiring what it felt, she looked over at him for one last scan of his eyes to check for any red flag energy, yet she only seen kindness there, so her hand went to work, rubbing the growing erection through his pants, stroking along it until it begged to be sprung free of its prison and held in hand, skin on skin. Jess obliged, pulling back Paul's pants and taking his cock out in her eager grasp. Her grip moved up and down it smoothly, with delicate hold, bringing a soft moan of enjoyment from Paul who laid his head back with eyes closed, fully embracing the good feeling. It didn't take long of feeling his hard cock in her hand for Jess to feel her pussy grow wet and her own desire grow stronger. She stood up, slid her own pants down and climbed on top of him as he gazed admiringly at her. His fingers reached out to massage her clit and slide inside her before he grabbed upwards with them, applying pressure on her g spot, bringing moans from her too. She gyrated against his hand, pushing down against his strong fingers for pressure on her sensual spot which soon had her legs quivering as she came quickly on his hand. That was it, the lust was intensely lit. She wanted him inside of her properly right then. Her mouth attacked his, lips locking in wild play as she easily slid down onto his waiting dick with her soaking pussy. Oh damn it felt good, feeling the hardness slide inside of her, deeper and deeper until she could go no lower, loving every inch she felt filling her up. As she enjoyed that incredible feeling, she nestled her face into Paul's neck, feeling his warm breath on hers as her kissed upon her skin. Jess started slowly bucking against him with his hard dick all the way inside her pussy, grinding out more and more pleasure with every gyrating movement, her hips working strong to pull him deeper inside, grinding his hardness against all the tender spots inside. His hands moved from her hips to under her top, up to her breasts. Her top was lifted up and bra undone before the warmth of his mouth moved to her breasts, kissing over them, taking her erect nipples into his mouth, one at a time, suckling softly , flicking his tongue over them inside his mouth. Uggghh, it feel amazing, caused her thrusting to pick up pace and passion as she began to ride him with powerful motion, each swing forward and back of her hips sending blasts of pleasure through her pussy, saturating her whole body with joy. She gripped his head in one of her hands pulled his mouth closer over her breasts as she bucked wild, wanted more and more of him in her. "Urgghhh fuck, fuck, bite my neck!"

Paul obliged, kissing and gently biting at the flesh of her throat which pushed her to the edge. "Ohhh, I'm COMING!"

She could feel it close, her pussy heated up like lava as she wildly pumped out a few more thrusts of her pussy grinding on his cock before she erupted, pleasure and heat spreading like wildfire through her pussy. She feel down against him, whole body shaking as her pussy gripped and unclenched around his dick, her chest heaving for breath, her mouth kissing his neck before her pussy relaxed around him. As her whole body relaxed after the pleasure, she noticed something move in the reflection of a mirror out of the corner of her eye. She swung head around to look at where that was in the room and for the tiniest fraction of a moment, it seemed as if there was a translucent, ghastly face silently screaming as lightning flashed around them. Jess screamed out as she fell off Paul, scrambled back across the couch. "ARGH!!"

Paul looked around frantically. "What? What is it?"

Jess yanked her pants back up, stood up to back away while staring at where she swore she seen the face. "There was.. I don't know.. I swear I seen like a face or ghost or someone there. It was horrifying!"

Paul got up to, pointed to where Jess was staring with wide frightened eyes. "There?"

She nodded. He walked over there, looked all around, even checked in the nearby room. "There's nobody there. Want me to check upstairs?"

Although she wasn't sure she wanted to be left alone downstairs, Jess nodded, then followed Paul half way up the stairs when he went all the way up. Between fearfully, constantly checking back behind her downstairs and looking around there, and keeping an eye on upstairs activity, Jess could hear and most of the time see Paul checking around the upstairs rooms. She thought she could hear multiple people moving around in one of the rooms he was in, but put it down to his cat being in there with him. As she waited, paranoia grew as a feeling intensified like someone or something was watching her standing there. It had her on edge, yet she was pushed to major nerves by cold presence she felt right by her, as if some unseen thing was right there next to her, just waiting to do something to her. It was too much, she had to get away from it, so she fled all the way upstairs to find Paul. Jess burst into the last room she seen him enter which is when fright hit her like a wrecking ball. There in the room was Paul, except a translucent, corpse, ghost version of him, just hovering in the middle of the room, staring back at her. Scream tried to come out of her, yet voice was frozen by fear. She managed to turn to try to flee, but was met by corpse, ghost Paul on the other side of the doorway. Heart thumping, legs turning to jelly, Jess staggered back into the bedroom as Paul advanced on her with undead ghoulish gaze. After only a few steps back, Jess fell over on the bed, crawled backwards until she found herself backed against the wall, too scared to move as Paul advanced on her. He grabbed at her legs with touch so cld she felt it through her pants.. the pants that he quickly tore off her along with her underwear. The fear had her feeling as if a heart attack was imminent, yet the adrenalin had her pussy wetter than it had been before. She offered little resistance as he parted her legs with chilly touch that had her trembling twice as much. He stroked his fingers up her thighs, grazing their coolness against the heat of her pussy as he kissed up her legs, working his way up to have his mouth at the center of her pleasure zone. His tongue was icey cold, yet felt incredible as it flicked against her burning hot clit causing an otherworldly sensation that fluttered all through her. Fear and pleasure clashed and combined as Jess was still too scared to move, yet also enjoying every second of it.. the feel of cool lips and tongue suckling on her clit while cold fingers penetrated hot pussy. Paul lapped at her clit with unhuman precision, flickering tongue with such speed, she felt orgasm rising quickly once more. Without thinking of doing it, she thrust her hips up to draw his tongue in harder against clit and fingers in deeper. With ass up in air, she fucked against what he did to her, yearning for what was coming. While still mouth fucking her, he used his free arm to lift her up off the bed, throw her up so her thighs wrapped around his face. It felt like she was floating in the air, held up by nothingness except the power of his tongue darting in to her pussy, stroking and twisting to prod against her g spot as if his tongue had a life of its own. It pressed and rolled against her g spot with such strength she couldn't help but buck against his face as that amazing feel spread through her once more. Then when he started pulled her crotch down against his face in time with her gyrating against it, it felt mindblowing. She could feel herself losing control and before she knew it, her pussy gushed orgasm into his waiting mouth as she screamed out with wild joy, pulling his head in as deep as she could while floating in the air. Before her pleasure convulsions could even stop, he dropped her down into his arms, span her around and shoved her, face first, up against the wall and shoved his cold but thick cock straight up her soaked pussy from behind. She felt completely helpless, pinned up against the wall, every thrust from him pressing her face against it harder, lifting her off the floor with powerful strokes. Her legs went numb from the power of it and the pleasure it gave, with each mighty thrust in and up bringing another orgasm, one after another, each exploding her pussy in pure thrill that had her breathless, almost completely numb all over except to the pleasure in he pussy. Paul grunted louder with each wild pump that almost felt like pussy was getting stretched so deep his cock might reach her stomach, lifting her up and slamming her against wall with such hungry passion. If it wasn't for his cock holding her up, she would have collapsed with weakness in the waves of orgasms that rocked her over and over, almost sending her unconscious. All of a sudden Paul got in real tight against her, his cold breath on her neck as she felt him unload inside of her, sperm shooting into her pussy as he gave one last powerful thrust that rocked her with such an orgasm she lost consciousness.

When she was finally woken later from the cracking of more thunder above, she sat up on the dust covered floorboards and looked around, rubbing her eyes in the dark. She struggled to her feet, pussy aching from the fucking she'd gotten and carefully moved around in the dark, trying to find something to grab ahold of to get bearings. It was when lightning flashed once again that she saw the room was completely empty, no bed, no furniture, just dust and cobwebs everywhere.

THE END

SUCCULENT PENETRATION 1 - EAT PREY, CUM

Jade was an ancient vampire who had grown tired of feeding on the blood of common beings. Even with her powers grown over centuries enabling her to go long periods without feeding, the taste of common blood still tasted rotten in her mouth, no matter how hungry she had grown. A solution had come to her though. One that required her to travel across countries in search of a target with rich enough blood she would finally be able to enjoy feasting again. Not only that, it had been such a long time since she'd fed on prey who'd really put up a fight, which was a difficult thing to find considering the level of power she'd grown. Sure some humans had been able to give a bit of a fight, but nothing that felt like a challenge or got her undead heart racing. Combining those two factors into it made it damn near impossible to find the right target, yet after what felt like endless research, she felt like she might have finally found one. Her target (Edwin) was a prince of a small European country but he'd also served in his country's military and even won an armed forces boxing title. All of that was accomplished before he'd turned 30 and he'd only grown into better physical shape since. There were even rumors he'd been working as a spy, surviving numerous death scenarios. Jade was practically frothing at the mouth as she travelled to Edwin's country to attend a gala held by his family at their royal estate. It hadn't been too hard for her to procure an invite using the many high level connections in the world she'd gathered over the years. The fact she was incredibly wealthy didn't hurt either. Now for a feed of this quality, with the high expectations she had, Jade really wanted to make the most of it, to savor the whole experience, so getting to know Edwin at the gala, getting into his head, taking in who he was, it all needed to happen before she could truly enjoy the hunt and feed. She wore a long red dress to the event which was split down the side to show off one of her long, smooth legs. It was also a good dress for showing off her bountiful cleavage that she needed no bra to keep upright thanks to her immortal body. Pretty young socialites from around the world crowded around Edwin, all trying to be the one to capture his heart, enchanted by his family's enormous wealth. His striking good lucks and athletic build helped add to their thirst too. All Jade had to do to grab his attention was slowly make her way round the grand room, ignoring the countless men who tried to strike up conversation with her or offer her drinks. She could have simply walked right up to Edwin and used her vampiric eye enchantment to make him her drooling lap dog like all the other men sought to be, but what was the fun or challenge in that? She came for sport and excitement, not fast food home delivered. She knew the man was a hunter by nature too, thinking and feeling much the same way which made the gaggle of thirsty women unattractive options to him apart from being easy one night stands who were quickly forgotten. No, his hunger and excitement was lit by the sight of the breathtakingly beautiful Jade ignoring some of the richest and handsomest men the surrounding countries had to offer, most of them dismissed with a wave of hand that showed she cared little for their status and was somehow above them all. Edwin knew he had to have her. That she was a prize he had to win, something he had to conquer, getting her to submit to his will. He waited until Jade had stopped moving so his conquest would be made easier before he walked away from the thirsty gaggle and approached her. He pretended to admire her dress by touching the fabric, running his fingers down her arm. "You look quite striking, mysterious angel. It's a beauty not from this part of the world though."

She smiled. "You've a good eye. If you've approached me for sport though, you must know, I never lose."

She punctuated that line with a playful wink. Edwin replied. "Who says either of us have to lose. I feel we're both winners. Glory can be shared."

She sipped on some wine before her free hand grazed against his. "Indeed we are, and it most certainly can, but this whole affair feels rather stuffy, don't you think? Easy pickings all around."

He boldly took her hand in his and said. "I do find fresh air gets the blood pumping fierce and soul invigorated. Shall we take a walk around the grounds?"

She slid her hand out of his. "So you can get me alone? Maybe take advantage of my lightheaded mood from your fine wine I've been drinking?"

He gave her a wink before striding away towards the exit. "I doubt you're so easily taken advantage of."

She smiled as she watched him go outside, even made him wait a few minutes before she too moved out there. She found him leaning against a tree, carving at a piece of wood with his pocket knife while he waited. Now that got her heart beat up a little as it was common knowledge that vampires were killed by stake through heart. She couldn't help but wonder if he knew her truth, yet the size of his carving was so little, it stood no real chance of breaching her ribcage and into heart. Even if it was his intention to stake her, she liked her chances of coming out victorious anyway. "Carving something to defend yourself from me incase I try to take advantage of you out here?"

Edwin chuckled, tossed the wood aside and slid his knife back into a pocket. "Just passing time. I can't remember the last time someone made me wait for them. Busy were you?"

"I see. Does that really matter?"

He shook his head. "Not really. We're out here together now. Shall I show you around the grounds?"

She led the way away. "To see statues of your ancestors and pretty flowers? Doesn't sound like something to get the blood pumping, does it?"

He followed her in the direction of the forest. "Agreed. The forest it is, if you don't mind that dress getting ruined."

She smirked at him as he caught up, walked close beside her. She said. "It's just material."

She took his hand in hers as they made their way off the grounds and into the forest where moonlight only peeked through in rare spots. As they made their way deeper in and further from society, she rubbed her thumb over his hand in hers and asked. "I bet you come out here often. You seem the adventurous type, not satisfied with being caged up with luxuries."

Before he could respond, she turned to him and planted a kiss on him that he happily accepted. It lasted just long enough to build some passion up as she stroked at his cock, feeling it grow hard under her hand. He reached down and under her dress through the side slit and was pleased to find she had no panties on. He rubbed at her clit with strong fingers as both moaned a little. He soon moved his hand to penetrate her pussy with fingers but before he could, she bit down on his bottom lip, drew a small amount of blood from him that she savored in her own mouth, licking it from her own lips. He gave her a push backwards, away from him. "B*tch! You want to get freaky? I'll show you freaky."

He advanced o her to take her in his grasp, have his way with her but she slipped passed him at the last moment. He spun around to seize at her again, yet could find no sight of her, just the sound of her giggling from the darkness. Her taunting whisper floated to him. Defeat me and I'm all yours to do with as you wish, fierce warrior."

What had been annoyance growing in him, turned to excitement upon hearing that and the sultry tone it was whispered in. He replied. "Don't get lost out there, devilish angel. Creatures roam that are almost as deadly as I. I would hate to find you devoured before I got my taste."

Amused laughter echoed around him before something swopped at his head, knocked him to the ground, bleeding from a fresh wound. "What the fuck?!"

He grabbed at a nearby fallen branch to use as self defense and leapt back to his feet, spinning around in search of whatever had attacked him. It didn't seem possible it could have been a bird of prey under that much tree coverage but that's the only thing he could accept as possibility. As he swirled, he caught the view of two glowing eyes up in the darkness of one of the trees. He stared harder to make out what it was. It soon became quite clear as it was Jade who leapt out of the tree, dived at Edwin with fangs bared and eyes glowing devilish red. He swung the branch at her as hard as he could, connecting with a thick thud against her head that sent her scurrying away in the blink of an eye upon landing near him. He shouted out. "What are you, monster?! Show yourself! Come on! You will be bested!"

As she watched him from the darkness behind, she felt invigorated, her pussy warming up for the first times in decades. Finally, a worthy foe. The wound on her head healed almost instantly as she stalked his movements, aroused and hungered by the fear his heart pumped, but also the courage he showed through it. She taunted him again. "Such a fine meal you'll make."

He swung out in the direction of her voice, yet she'd already moved around again, fangs dripping with primal hunger, pussy just as wet. He roared. "Come and feast then, devil! You won't get this easy th.."

His words were cut short by Jade tackling him to the ground and swatting the branch out of reach. The scuffled on the ground for a few moments as he tried to fight back, yet soon found himself pinned down with her sitting on top of him. His face red, angered at being beaten, yet also fearing for his life, he hissed. "Monster!"

She shrugged. "I've been called worse."

Jade bared her fangs and leant down to bite into Edwin's neck, yet was met with a mighty headbutt from him that temporarily broke her nose, blurred her vision a little for a few moments. She screamed at him, broke one of his arms and used her free hand to push his head sideways, exposing his neck where she planted her fangs into his flesh, drawing blood and life into her mouth with incredible, but patient thirst. The warm blood flowing into her mouth tasted divine, like life itself coursing through her, pumping through her own heart and body, making her feel alive again. As she feasted on his writhing and howling self, she could feel his cock grow hard against her, which impressed her considering the blood she was taking from him. Knowing she had him in a weak enough state he had no chance of escaping, she used one hand to tear his pants open before she hiked her dress up and slid her pussy down onto his cock, sliding all the way down it as he bucked and roared. "NO! GET OFF ME, DEVIL!"

His frantic writhing only served to bring more pleasure to her as his hardened cock thrashed wildly into her pussy as he tried to break free from her. She leant down again to kiss him with her blood stained lips, yet he turned his head sideways to escape it. She shook her head. "Tsk tsk. You're mine now. Just enjoy it."

She grabbed his head and forced her lips onto his, pressing her tongue into his mouth as she rode his frantic motions with expert agility, using his fear to enhance her pleasure. She wanted to feast on more of his blood, yet was enjoying him having some strength remaining to writhe underneath her, trying to fight back instead of being meek, defeated prey. He bit at her tongue, drawing blood from her that dripped into his mouth which riled her up even more. "Oh you bad man!"

She increased the pace of her hips pumping her pussy on dick before lunging at his throat again, penetrating his flesh with fangs again which brought a weird howl of pained pleasure from him. She made sure to drink on his blood slowly while taking his dick in passionately, moving in beautiful scary unison with his panicked thrusts, their bodies combining in perfect fear and joy. The more of his blood she drank, the warmer her pussy got around his cock. The sensual feeling of fangs in his neck and warm pussy fucking his dick had him enjoying it the erotic feeling of it all, the pleasure overwhelming the fear of death, or at least having him thinking it would be an incredible way to go out. He started kissing her neck too, gently biting at her skin between sucks and kisses of her flesh. His good hand ran up her back, stroked through her hair before their mouths locked once again in messy, bloody pleasure, tongues and lips dancing a deadly game as bodies moved together, gyrating and pumping together. Jade tore her dress open at the chest, exposing her breasts before she pulled Edwin's mouth up to them. He eagerly accepted the task, sucking on her nipples as she pushed her hips back and forward, working his cock with moist passion. "Fucking bite them!"

Starting to feel a little woozy, but still completely enjoying the experience, he did what she asked, pinching his teeth upon one of her nipples and tugging at it which brought howls of joy out of her that would have scared any nearby animals away. Her nails dug into his back as she grinded pussy hard down against cock, feeling the firmness of his meat pressing all along her pussy walls. Blood trickled out of her nipple which caused her even more excitement. She switched fucking mode from grinding to bouncing up and down on his dick, rubbing her own clit as she did as he tried to keep mouth on breasts but failed. She shoved his head back down against the ground and she sprung up and down on top of him, each downward motion jamming his hard knob against the back of her vagina which jolted her entire self with hits of pleasure that almost caused her, in lust and passion, to drive fangs down into him again and devour what remained of his life. With fangs bared she stared down at him with glowing eyes, barely containing her thirst, wanting to at least orgasm before she finished him off. Her entire self felt a warmth she'd forgotten possible as each bounce upon his dick pushed her closer and closer to a powerful climax she ached for. He looked terrified of the expressions she showed in the midst of their passions, yet still somehow so damn sexy also. His vision started to blur a little as she fucked and fed the life out of him, yet the connection and eroticism was so powerful, blood remained in his dick that kept her pushing upon it with more and more hunger for the payoff moment. Whenever he started to look like he might lose consciousness, she slapped him hard across the face or dug her nails in deeper into his flesh to snap hi out of it. "Show me how strong you are, mortal man! Take me all the way like a powerful being should!"

Edwin shook off the drowsiness, grabbed ahold of Jade's hips and began thrusting upwards into her with all of his remaining strength, smashing penis in pussy as pussy drove down hard against it, each thrust making Jade squeal out in joy. She could feel herself so close to cuming, she flung her mouth down, fangs deep into Edwin's throat and sucked his blood out with incredible thirst as her hips moved with supernatural power and speed on top of him. Blood flowed out of him, into her mouth and down her body, sending warm sensation right through her right as vampiric pussy tightened up, gripping ahold of mortal cock as she climaxed around it. Overwhelming eruption of pleasure swept through her, caused her to howl in joy up at the sky with blood dripping from mouth over her pert, exposed breasts and hard nipples. She felt the closest to alive she'd been since being turned into a vampire so long ago. Breasts heaved as her body shook and breath blew hard until finally the waves of joy in pussy calmed down and she glanced back at the mortal man she'd ridden and fed on to that amazing feeling. He laid there, eyes rolled back in head, completely pale, not breathing at all and it was then that she started to care if he died, wanting to take that pleasure from his again and again, whenever she saw fit, whenever the cravings struck. She bit her fangs into her own wrist and let some of her supernatural blood flow into his mouth which soon worked to heal his mortal body from what she'd taken from it. He wouldn't turn into a vampire, well unless he fed on the life of another mortal, but Jade wasn't going to let that happen, no. She would keep him as her mortal plaything for as long as he remained useful to her.

THE END

YOUNG WOLF STYLE 1 - THE BEAST GETS IN

Grace was looking forward to her son Chris visiting for the first time since he'd left for college, maybe even a little more excited because he was bringing his best friend Daniel with him. Grace had met Daniel a couple of times when she'd gone to visit Chris at college and there had been an instant unspoken attraction between her and her son's best friend. It was obvious in the way he looked at her that he was thinking about all the things he wanted to do to her. Grace lived in a small town so usually when someone looked at her like that, it just creeped her out as they were people she wasn't attracted to at all. Yet Daniel was a strapping young man, full of life with natural, raw good looks that didn't involve any of that modern primping and styling so many men do to look good. There had been many an occasion where Daniel was involved in the fantasies Grace pictured while using her vibrator on herself, letting it sit upon her clit, taking her to powerful climaxes as she pictured Daniel lusting after her, and she blowing his mind with all the sexual things she could teach him. The sex she had with her husband (Chris' father Bruce) had grown stale, boring and become a chore, so the thought of all the passion and intensity the young Daniel would bring to the bed (or other more fun places) got Grace hornier than she'd been in years. She would never act on the desires of course, apart from by herself masturbating, as it would be inappropriate to make a move on her son's friend. But if Daniel made the right moves on her, well that could likely be a different story. Chris' father wasn't home when they arrived late on the Friday. He never was actually as he'd spend many nights with his friends either at games, or playing poker or whatever the truth was about what he was doing that he didn't tell Grace. She didn't give a shit anymore really. When Chris and Daniel arrived, it was obvious instantly that Daniel was still hot for her as she felt his heartbeat race when she gave him a hug hello. His hand lingered on her back, slid down to her lower back before he let go of the hug. Grace gave him a warm smile. "Good to see you again Daniel."

He smiled back. "You too Mrs Jones. Thanks for letting me crash for the weekend too."

"That's fine hun. You can either have the couch or get Chris to blow up the air mattress for you."

"Cool, thanks Mrs.."

She touched his arm, "Call me Grace, hun. All that Mrs talk adds twenty years to me."

He gave a nod. "Okay Grace, my bad."

Their eye contact lingered long enough that Chris started to get weirded out by it. "Come on dick, we need to get ready."

Grace asked. "You two going out? Catching up with old friends?"

Chris replied. "Yeah, something like that. We'll be out late so don't get into stress mode about it."

"That's fine, just don't be drunk calling at 3am for a lift home. Call an uber like your father does. Here's some money for it."

"Thanks mom."

Later that night, with the house to herself and a bottle of wine being defeated, Grace binged Santa Clarita Diet on Netflix. She heard a scratching at one of the living room windows which snapped her out of her peaceful bliss, got her jumping up to look over at the window. Heart raced and fingers clenched but she saw nothing there. No tree or branch was even remotely close to the window though which kept her right on edge. She grabbed ahold of the wine bottle to use in self-defense if necessary. "Hello? Is someone there?   That better not be you messing around Chris, I swear! Or you Bruce!"

There was no response and also no way in hell she was going to unlock the door and go outside to check. Nope. That was just asking for trouble. She did slowly approached the window though to peek out from a safe enough distance back from it. She couldn't see anyone out there from her view. Heart pumping hard, she inched a little closer for a better look with fingers tight around the bottle when there was a loud thump on the roof and heavy scurrying that damn near gave her a heart attack. It sounded way too loud to be a possum or cat. She backed up panicked to the middle of the room and grabbed her phone, fumbled to dial Chris to see if it was him messing with her. He answered but his voice was drowned out by the sounds of a party around him before the connection cut out. She tried calling back but his phone was turned off or battery had died. She didn't know. Grace swung around and around, fearful she might be attacked from behind at any moment when more rooftop scurrying nearly caused her to jump out of her own skin with fright. She shouted out, trying to sound scary herself, yet let down by the fear in her voice. "WHO'S THERE?! I'M CALLING THE POLICE!"

She did start to call the police yet stopped when she saw something crash passed a window from above and thud into the ground below. She shrieked, jumping backwards, almost dropped the bottle, did drop her phone which turned it off. "ARGH! What the fuck?!"

She scrambled for her phone to call the police, yet every moment it took to load up felt like hours as she could hear something moving around outside of the window. Groans of pain soon touched at Grace's compassion through her fear, had her move back to the window to see if someone was badly hurt and needed help. She got a pleasant shock when she seen Daniel out there, naked, struggling up to hands and knees, his impressive cock swinging between his legs as he did. Grace felt hot, peaked by the sight of the naked young man outside her window, yet worry kicked in quickly. She rushed outside to see if he was okay and needed help, yet when she got around to that side of the house, all she saw there was a giant wolfbeast bounding on all fours out of the yard. With a shriek Grace tossed the wine bottle at it before it bounded over a fence.

Chest heaving, she looked around for Daniel in fear he'd been attacked by the beast, yet she couldn't see him anywhere. Fear struck harder as she had the thought that maybe the beast had eaten him or something like that. It hadn't looked like it was carrying him away. She looked around more, calling out his name, yet there were no signs of blood or any struggle really, just some tufts of wolf hair and large paw prints in the ground. Fearing the beast could return at any moment and with no sight of Daniel anywhere, Grace rushed back into her home, locked the door behind her and went to call the police again. She heard the sound of heavy steps outside right before the front door smashed in as the giant beast crashed through. It lunged at Grace, knocking her to the ground, pinning her there with powerful paw on chest as it pushed its mouth right I close to her throat, hot breath on her skin. She was too terrified to scream or move or do anything except close her eyes and hope it was all a wine induced nightmare. The sound of cracking and howls of pain above her had her trembling, petrified, yet when the weight of pressure holding her down got lighter then lifted off, she managed to barely open one eye to peek out. Another pleasant surprise was had when she seen Daniel, naked again, standing over her. He backed away in shame as she stood up, not being able to help glancing down at his cock. He held hands up in apology. "I'm so sorry, i.. I.."

She stood up too, moved closer to him, studying him. "That was you? The wolf beast?"

He nodded. "Yes, I'm.. I didn't mean to hurt you, I'm so sorry Grace."

She moved closer to him, went around him and closed the broken door as best she could before she returned attention to her son's best friend standing naked in front of her. He shivered which prompted her to grab the blanket from the couch before letting the million questions she had pour out. As she wrapped the blanket around him, her hands brushed over his flesh. They stood there, face to face, eye contact held as his panting breathing calmed down. She touched at his face. "What are you? A werewolf?"

He nodded. "That's my best guess. I got attacked on a road trip earlier this year and this has been happening to me a few nights a month ever since. Usually I can control it better, take myself out somewhere isolated when I turn, but this time.."

He looked longingly at Grace, leaning in a little closer to her and she leant in closer too. Her hands moved under the blanket, over his toned stomach, up his chest and over his pecs. He leant in to kiss her, but she put a finger up to his lips. "Not yet."

One of her hands ran up the back of his head, pulled his face down to her neck where his lips pressed against her flesh, kissing and sucking, tugging at her skin with wet mouth which had her shivering in delight. As he made oral love to her tender neck, she whispered. "Use your teeth a little."

He obliged, gently, playfully tugging at neck with teeth which brought a moan from Grace as she took his erect bone in one of her hands, stroked it gently and slowly, back and forth, running her fingers and palm up and down it. This got him breathing heavy against her neck which turned her on even more. He had been clumbsily fumbling at her breasts and nipples during this but she took of his hands and guided it to her clit where she controlled the movement of his fingers there until he was rolling her clit between fingers just how she liked it. Grace moaned. "Oh yes."

She then held his head back up and started kissing him with fiery passion. His passion was a bit amateur though, a little too slopping for her liking so she stopped and said. "Easy wolfy. Make tender love with your mouth, don't try and eat my face with it. He gave a nod of understanding before she started kissing him again. The loner they kissed, the quicker the motion on her button got which in turn increased the power of her strokes on his cock. It'd been a long time since she'd been with a young person, but she remembered the signals from when she was young that a male was getting close to erupting. Her hand let go of his cock and pulled his hand tighter against her pussy, guiding fingers inside her while pressing the palm against her clit, putting rubbing pressure on it with every movement of his fingers inside her warmness. He grunted. "I wanna fuck you so bad. I have for so long."

She slapped him with one hand while holding his other in place on her pussy. "You'll wait a bit longer."

Still hand fucking her, his breathing intensified and body starting changing a little, muscles bulged along his arms, shoulders and back, body grew hairier and k9 teeth extended. Grace got a bit worried he was going to go full beast transformation and lose control, but he stopped himself from transforming into full beast so he remained mostly human apart from those slight changes, including big tongue licking lips. Grace ran her hands over his newly formed muscles, up to his head and said. "Eat the cat to earn the prize, wolfy."

Panting, all worked up, Daniel dropped down onto all fours which made his muscles transform even more before he started lapping with big powerful tongue at Grace's clit and pussy, bringing squeals of delight from her as she ran her hands through his thick hair. Every lap of bit wet tongue splashed pleasure sensation through her pussy. "Aw yes! Lap it up, wolfy!"

His mouth went crazy on her pussy, lapping it up like a fresh bowl of water on a hot day. The stokes of his big tongue were so powerful and it had been so long since she'd had another person service her, she was cuming in no time at all, pulling his mouth deeper as she exploded orgasm into it. Her legs shook from the powerful pleasure eruption, caused them to give way beneath her. Daniel caught her in his muscled up arms and lifted her off the ground. She stoked his face and said. "Now you get to fuck. Just don't come too quick, bad boy."

He carried her over to the wall and stood her up against it, lifted up one of her legs, bent down a little and stood back up, pushing his cock into her pussy with eager momentum. Grace cried out a little and smacked him over the head. "Easy!"

He nodded and began slowly thrusting up inside her with as careful a speed as his young, wild self could manage, which wasn't exactly tender, although he was lucky Grace started to get juicier down there as he licked and panted on her neck. She felt incredible having dick inside her again, feeling that passion, true excitement as if she was a young woman embracing the fun in life once more. As Daniel held one of her legs up, he used the other to reach down and twiddle her clit while pumping cock into pussy. Grace shrieked. 'Oh yes! Good boy!"

She kissed him passionately. Their mouths dueled and tongues battled in loving tango as each pump he gave her shot rippling sensations through her. She knew it wouldn't be long before she came again, yet by Daniel's grunting and panting, the look in his eyes, she knew he was closer. Grace shoved him backwards. "Not yet, stud."

He growled with wild desire, strode towards her with cock throbbing to get what it needed. He was met with another slap though. "Get on the floor!"

He happily obeyed, lying down on his back as Grace climbed on top of him, pinched his nipples while inserting his dick back in her pussy. She grabbed a handful of his chest hair and twisted it which made him howl out so primally. She said. "This is what happens if I see you about to cum before me. Understood?"

Once more, he nodded. She leant down, kissing his neck as she gyrated back and forth on his cock, even biting his neck at times as she did which brought little howls of pleasure from his. She grinded slowly, working herself patiently towards the big explosion she wanted, while also trying to keep him from blowing too quickly. As she thrust hips back and forth, feeling every inch of his cock sliding along her pussy, she kissed up his neck and back to his mouth. She could feel it building again, getting herself closer. His excitement grew too as he started thrusting his hips to meet her movements. It felt so fucking good but she had to keep control. She bit his tongue and moaned. "I'll tell you when you can fuck."

He moaned back. "Yes queen."

"Aw fuck."

She moaned again and climbed off him, got on her hands and knees with her ass and pussy pointed at him. "Unleash, wolfy. Finish this off."

He almost fell flat on his face scrambling to get to her so excitedly, but remembered wheat she had already told him before he made the mistake of wildly just plunging in again. He grabbed her by the hips and slowly slid inside her before beginning deep but slow thrusts. She looked back. "I said unleash!"

His hip fucking, pussy fucking, dick thrusting power and speed stepped up a whole lot of levels as he went wild at Grace's pussy, pumping with everything he had to please his master. Every thrust sent shockwaves through her, knocking her forward more and more with each pump, yet the power of his thrusts slid him forward each time too, keeping her pussy wrapped around his bone as she wailed and moaned, barely able to keep herself from collapsing under the weight of the pleasure and the supernatural might of his dick. She tensed up as it happened, her pussy climaxing in glorious explosion, gripping upon his cock with such intense convulsions he came too fountaining his load into her quivering pussy. She screamed out in joy as he howled primal, gripping tight on her hips, holding pussy right there to take all of his load until not a drop was left. The twitching of pussy calmed down, bringing a contented sigh from Grace who laid down on the floor, exhausted, content. She pulled Daniel over to her, made him cuddle up with her, enjoying the warmth of his body heat against her. "Good boy."

THE END

BLESSED BANGS 1 - HOLY SEED

Kayla was walking home one night after a quick trip to the corner store for some snacks to binge watch Netflix with. She passed by a church when a loud commotion coming from inside the place of worship caught her attention. Worried about putting herself in danger, she thought about just ignoring it and getting home quicker, calling the police, yet a shout of pain from inside had her rush to a window to peer in to see if someone needed help. What she saw inside, at first it looked like two men fighting. It soon became clear this was no standard battle though as one of the men attacked and defended with glowing light moves and sprouted wings from back to avoid some of the strikes from the other. The other man attacked with moves of fire and monsterish facial expressions that caused Kayla to drop her ice-cream and chocolate coated cookies in frightened shock. As fire and light collided in epic duel, a possibly fatal blow was struck on the being of light from the being of fire that pierced midriff with scorching sharpness. The man of light fell back as if defeated which brought the monsterish being of fire leaping at him to finish him. Kayla shrieked for the winged man of light. The creature of fire came down hard out of air to strike finishing blow on man of light yet was instead met with a blade of light that sliced through him, cause him to burst into fiery ash, gone. Even after all the unbelievable things she'd just witnesses, that had her doubting if she was actually awake in the real world or just dreaming. The sight of the winged being bleeding out on the church floor, in desperate need for help had Kayla acting on instinct, compassion. She dashed inside to help him without a thought for what could happen to herself. She found him crashing back down to floor after using wings to rise up, yet lacking the strength to stay up. He hit the floor with a pained howl that got her rushing even quicker to him, despite how in awe she'd been seeing him fly up like he did, majestic glowing wings catching moonlight through window. Kayla reached him, touched his arm as she glanced at the bleeding wound. "Hey, just rest, okay. I'll call an ambulance."

He gripped her arm too, stared deep into her eyes with his own that flickered light in pupil. His touching of her sent a beautiful feeling of warmth coursing through her body and mind, like nothing she'd ever experienced before. "No. No others. You can help me."

"Me? But how? I'm not a doctor or anything like that. You need.."

He replied I such a calm, comforting tone. "Kayla.. it's okay. Do you have somewhere I can rest?"

"Well yes, but.."

His hand gently rubbed her arm as his eyes showed a deep soul kindness that showed her she could trust him. She said. "Okay. Let's get you to my place. It's just a few buildings away."

She helped him to his feet, not even wondering how he knew her name, just that it felt right. As she supported his body weight to her place, she asked. "So um, what do I call you? And oh, just wondering.. what the heck happened in there? What was the thing and what are you? Are you an.."

He replied with calm tone, despite the obvious pai he was in. "An angel? I am, and the being you witnessed me battling with was a demon who had planned to sacrifice men of god in that church. Oh, and you can call me Lail if you like."

Nodding while trying to process all of that information, Kayla said. "Mhmm, mmhmm, I see. Well it's nice to meet you Lail. Umm.. there won't be any other demons coming revenge style or anything will there?"

"No Kayla, we're safe now. I could feel it if there were any more of them anywhere nearby. I wouldn't let any harm come to you, sweet soul."

"Thank you, Lail, I appreciate that. This is my place here."

After getting him up to her apartment, Kayla laid Lail down on her couch before fetching some bandages to wrap up his wounds. As she tended to his bare stomach, her fingers traced over the toned muscle definition of his abs and pecs. "So do angels need to hit the gym or do you just get this body naturally through holy powers or something?"

Lail grinned. "We are blessed beings, but I do look after myself."

Kayla grinned back. "I can tell."

Lail ran his hand down Kayla's arm. "You're pretty impressive yourself. So many humans have such dull energies, but you.. you have this powerful beauty."

They way he gazed at her combined with the warmth in his words made her believe it completely, despite having never thought much of her own looks or soul beauty or anything like that. She suddenly started to feel a warmth in her pussy that she hadn't felt since reading the Mortal Instruments books. "You'd probably be more comfortable and heal quicker in my bed instead of this old couch."

Smiling warmly, Lail leant in closer and whispered with warm breath by her neck and ear. "As long as you're in it with me."

Tingling sensation ran down her body from where his breath touched her skin and got her pussy heating up quickly. She eagerly helped him back to his feet yet before she could help carry him to the bedroom, he wrapped his arm around her and with one burst of his wings, flew them both into the room and onto the bed. He made sure that they landed with her on top of him so she wouldn't feel any impact from the landing except his hardening cock against her. With precision agility he managed to make sure his hard bulge pressed against her clit through her pants which brought a delighted shriek from her on feeling that firmness press on her love button. Kayla gawked at him with half delighted, half intrigued expression, pondering whether he meant to do that or not, before she decided she really didn't care. She started grinding her hips back and forth, rubbing her clit against his dick while keeping eye contact with him. He reached out, caressing her face as she did, feeling his cock grow harder, feeling a powerful heat spark between them. She could feel the length of his shaft as she guided her clit along it, back and forth, rubbing hard against every inch of it, all the way up to feeling his big knob hit her clit which sent ripples of sensual pleasure through her. Murmurs of enjoyment escaped both of them in groans and moans as she continued riding the outline of his cock, making herself wetter with every movement, slowly increasing pace as she worked herself closer to getting that amazing payoff feeling. He was entranced by it, by her passionate movements, the beautiful expressions of joy and determination on her face. He lifted her top off over her head and threw it away before leaning up and pressing mouth to her neck which brought more delighted noises from her, sped her pace up a bit more. "Arrrhh, yes!"

While still grinding her clit along his hard dick, she pulled his head down to her exposed breasts, guided his mouth onto her nipples which he started taking turns sucking on, tweaking each between lips and tongue, rolling them with oral warmth and pulling gently on them with teeth with a careful passion that got Kayla bucking as hard as she could against him. She could feel herself so close to coming, and he could sense it too. With a small burst of his wings, he thrust them both up into the air above the bed which gave a powerful push of cock against clit that took her over the edge, feeling her pussy explode as they were in mid-air. Her legs wrapped around him as her groin convulsed a mighty orgasm out of her that had her squeezing around his crotch with fierce tremors. She was literally floating on air, as well as figuratively from the glowing in her pussy. They fell gently back down to the bed with her on top. She collapsed down contently with her head on his chest. Lail stroked her head, ran his fingers through her hair, kissed her forehead as she cuddled up to him, satisfied. Kayla deliriously mumbled. "That was incredible."

Lail said back. "You made it so, beautiful soul."

Smiling, she looked up at him and planted a soft, sweet kiss on his lips that he embraced and returned, their mouths making slow love in blissful moments. Despite the horniness, both felt tired after their own exertions of that night.. Kayla from the carrying him around and putting that energy into dry fucking herself to orgasm on him.. him from the battle he had with the demon and needing to heal from the wounds. They fell asleep right there in each other's arms, cuddled up cozy, content, although keen for what might happen when they woke with more energy. Warm daylight poured into the room and glowed over them by the time they both awoke. His wounds were all but fully healed from the battle the night before. Smiles spread on both of their faces as they stared at each other. Both knew what they wanted to happen next, yet Kayla felt a little scared at the thought of actually fucking an angel. She had no idea what might happen during it or because of it, so she got up, headed to the kitchen. "Ima cook you something. I hope you like spicy omelettes."

"Have you got fruit?"

Kayla tapped her own head. "Right, right, makes sense an angel would be vegetarian, yeah? Not consuming things that have life?"

Lail followed her out of the bedroom. "Yes, something like that."

As she started slicing some mango up for him, he stood behind her with hands around her, kissed her neck. There is some flesh I enjoy tasting though. She could feel his erect cock pressing against her ass so she gave it a gentle backwards grind as she placed some grapes in the bowl with the mango. 'Mmm, I bet there is. I bet you're bursting for some more of it after last night's bit of fun. You're a gentleman for letting me fall asleep after that by the way. Mortal males wouldn't have that self-control or decency."

He slid his hand up over her belly button, tracing his fingers over her stomach. "Well, I am an angel."

Then he slid his hand down her pants. "Angels have needs too though."

As he slid a finger inside her and rubbed her g spot, she moaned and fed him a juicy piece of mango. He patiently enjoyed the tasty fruit while pulling up against Kayla's g spot. Moaning, being lifted up onto the tips of her toes, she reached back and slid her hand down his pants. She took a hold of his prick which felt so warm in her hand and started running her hand up and down it as he massaged her pleasure spot. His free hand reached up to her breasts, started pinching her nipples and rolling them between finger tips which made them perky and extra sensitive. She shivered, rested her head backwards against his chest. "Ohhh baby, fuck!"

As both massaged each other into wonderful pleasure, his finger inside of her warmth, her hand stroking up and down his mighty member, she tilted her head back and reached to kiss him which he moved to embrace, lips locking again and tongues crashing against each other in midst of moans of pleasure. His holy cock ached to be set free from his pants and Kayla obliged it, set it loose which enabled her to work it with greater space and passion. With eyes closed, she hadn't even realized they were floating in the air again as his palm on her pussy had helped lift her up. She yanked his pants down the rest of the way so they fell off which made him do the same thing to her. Kissing along his face, desperate to feel his rod inside her hungry pussy, she moaned. "Take me! Take me however angels do. However you want!"

Lail needed no further prompting. He kissed her again with deep tenderness before he laid her down on the kitchen bench, threw her legs over his shoulders as he floated in the air and smoothly slid his blessed beef into the welcoming warmth of her love hole. Pleasure rippling through her with each thrust and inch he went deeper into her, Kayla grabbed one of his hands and moved it to her throat. He squeezed a little, just enough to give her what she wanted which had her half gasping, half groaning in joy while the hardness of his holy dick moved with powerful grace along her vagina, touching every sensitive nerve and spot with powerful blessing that had her trembling in his grasp. She whimpered. "Ha.. harder!"

Lail needed not to be asked twice, so he began using his wings to drive himself deeper into her with every thrust.. his holy ability ramming pleasure coursing through her. "Oh god yes, fuck!"

She spasmed in the enjoyment of it, thrashing around, sending the bowl of fruit sailing off the bench and crashing on the floor.. the juice of the spilt mango nothing compared to how wet her pussy had gotten. His cock glowed light and rippled power inside of her that had her vagina feeling like it was giving life to the universe, birthing a sun, falling in love with bursts of pure energy radiating inside of her. Every time he drove harder into her with wing powered thrust, it felt like a sunrise inside her which made her whole body glow and feel warm. She started to sweat, causing her body to slide back and forth on the counter as Lail pounded into her. Her toes curled up behind his head as pumped with intense passion, loving the sight of her eyes rolling back in her head from the insane pleasure he gave her. He cracked the counter top with a mighty thrust that would have sent her sliding off the bench if it wasn't for his hand on her throat that kept her pussy locked onto his cock. Seeing the damaged he did to the counter, he lifted Kayla up off it into the air with him, dropped her legs around him to be wrapped around his waist and pulled her up to be face to face with him, straddling him with tight but quivering legs, driving pussy deeper onto cock. She smashed their mouths together once again and bit his bottom lip, tugging at it as she bucked against his rod, using her legs to pull tight on his ass to drive penis deeper. She drew blood from his lip as her glistening body pressed against his glowing skin, not letting go, not with teeth nor pussy as she wanted that grand climax, the angel sperm unleashed inside of her, that holy explosion to erupt both of them in pleasure. The wounding of his flesh had him feeling peaked arousal as his hand on her throat had done to her so they both found themselves moaning, grinding, kissing, making all types of primal noises as their sweaty bodies clashed and colluded in incredible feeling. She slapped him as she felt them both getting close. "You going to give me that angel sperm? Huh?!"

"You want it? You want my holy seed? You think you can handle it?"

"urrggg, fucking give it to me! Give it to me nouurggghh."

She wrapped her arms around his head, pulled it tight to her chest as her pussy lit up like spring after winter, pleasure budding into beautiful orgasm that massaged his dick with her orgasmic pulsations. That was all that was needed to send him over the edge too as he groaned and tensed up with her, unloaded burst after burst of pure sperm inside her glowing pussy, his cock illuminating her love hole, the shared orgasm causing them both to glow brightly as they floated there in the air, clinging tightly to each other as. Panting with heavy breath, she pressed her forehead to his as she enjoyed the feel of his hot sperm rocketing into her vagina, feeling so blessed and satisfied. "That was fucking amazing."

He kissed her. "You're fucking amazing."

They slowly drifted back down to earth, still in each other's arms, still holding sweet eye contact. Her legs felt weak from the orgasm as she touched down, but he held her upright in his strong arms. Smiling, she asked. "So how does that work? I mean, can angels get humans pregnant?"

"If the connection is true, the feeling between hearts, souls and bodies pure, yes."

Kayla grinned. "One more thing."

"Yes, sweet queen."

She looked over to where the shower and bathroom was. "Are you as good with your mouth and tongue as you are with cock and wings?"

THE END

SUPER SPIT ROAST 1 - THE ORGASMERS

My name is Sasha, and for years I've been part of a team full of superpowered beings from all around the earth, as well as off it. Now back at the start, I was the only female in the squad and almost the only one without powers or high tech weapons and armor, yet I had something they all wanted. The uber soldiers, the gods, the billionaires, all of them were putty in my hands, weak at their knees whenever I felt like giving them a certain look, or a touch on arm, or even posed in a certain fight stance. I could see it in all of their eyes, they fantasized about having their way with me and the longer I resisted their flirtations, the more it drove them crazy. I fucking loved it, how powerful it made me feel having those powerful beings lusting after me, doing whatever I asked of them. It felt so good I thought I might never give in to the temptation.. that was until the first alien invasion almost defeated us and took over the world. When we survived that.. when we sealed that victory that saved the world, I knew it was time. I'd grown pretty close to James, Boss USA (the original uber soldier) since we'd been working together in the early days and there'd always been strong physical attraction between us, even if I'd never admitted it to him so I knew if it was any of them I gave into desire with, it'd be him. What was new though, was how wet Mike (Michael, Steel Soldier, the man of futuristic armor) had started making me since he made the sacrifice play that ended the alien invasion and almost cost him his life. The day dreams of those two powerful men taking me at the same time had me having to give my supersuit extra cleans. It also had me taking breaks in the middle of training to give my hot clit such a flicking as I fantasized about their strong cocks entering me in whatever holes they wanted, filling me up with their heroic seed like I was the greatest conquest of their lives. Even while plunging fingers into myself as thumb worked clit, I could almost feel their breath on my neck, their sweat on my skin. I had to have them, and soon. All worries about what it might do to the harmony of the team were forgotten as I made my way to the dining area where I knew they'd be after training. The place had so many amazing chefs to cook us whatever we wanted thanks to the billions of Mike. I was first there but it wasn't long before the others started entering, hunger worked up thanks to intense workout that made us all sexually charged even more. I made sure I made eye contact with James so he came and sat with me at the table I was at. I gave him a greeting hug, pressed my breasts firmly against him as I did while breathing on his neck. "You look good Boss. You been lifting extra in the gym lately?"

I could feel his heartbeat increase as I held him close, running my hand down his strapping arm as I pulled away from the hug, yet rubbed my leg against his under the table. His usual all American grin shone a little flushed this time as he replied, while holding deep eye contact, perhaps trying to figure out if I was fucking with him or trying to FUCK with him. "Have to be the best I can be. Limits are made to be broken."

His leg rubbed against mine as our eyes remained fixated on each other. Perhaps he was starting to realize what my body was trying to tell him. I wanted to grab his cock right then and there, feel it grow hard in my hands. Instead I felt his hand on my leg first, slowly moving fingers up along my thigh as his glowing smile had my heart fluttering, starting to make me all wet again. I was about to whisper something filthy in his ear when Mike sat down at the table with us. "You'd think you'd be able to tell which is better between a 5 star chef cooked burger and a cheap fast food burger, but shit, I'm thinking we should get a burger king or maccas in here. Don't tell Salter I said that though."

Even as Mike spoke, James' fingers smoothy moved up my thigh to between my legs where his strong fingers found and massaged my clit through the fabric of my supersuit. It took all of my will power not to let a moan out as warmth rapidly grew in my pussy, wishing James' fingers would just tear through the suit and penetrate me like I knew he so easily would be able to. Struggling to hold control in the situation, I forced my self to look at Mike and say. "I thought you were on a juice cleanse. Only putting healthy things in your body. Healthy body, healthy mind and all that."

Despite how hard I was trying to hide the pleasure I was feeling from James' fingers moving firmer and faster on my clit, Mike quickly picked up on the vibe going on. His eyes glanced downwards for a moment, as if he could see through the table before his foot started playing with mine. "Sometimes what is put in your body can just be about fun."

Oh fuck, I couldn't help myself. As I could feel an orgasm building in my pussy, the heat growing through my body, I shot my hand over to Mike's crotch and grabbed ahold of his cock, started massaging it through his pants, feeling it grow big and hard in the palm of my hand. Both men were aware of what was going on with the other. Mike managed to keep a cool look and keep eating as I stroked his big cock under the table while James' fingers worked me to closer and closer to cuming right there. I couldn't concentrate on conversation anymore, was doing all I could not to just collapse back against the booth backing with eyes closed to fully enjoy the experience. Wanting that pleasure explosion to come and James to not lose interest, I slipped my free hand under the table and straight down his pants, took ahold of his dick that felt like nothing I'd ever touched before. It was harder than pulsanium metal and bulged out of his pants in my hand. I would need four hands to control that monster but one had to do for the time being. I stroked my hand up and down his hard dick with expert movements that made up for the lack of size of my hand to his dick. Fuck, I so badly wanted both of their cocks out in the open right then so I could go nuts on them, using all of my agility to make them feel amazing so they would take me with unrivaled passion. As my hands started getting both of them breathing a little heavier, I could feel it coming, the volcanoing of my pussy building up to erupt soon. As if he could tell it,

James ripped a hole in my pants with his fingers and slid two up inside me to rub my gspot while his thumb continued working my clit. That was all I fucking needed to take me over the edge as I thrust my hips closer to his hand, cuming fiercely with incredible waves of pleasure that had my whole body shaking. I couldn't help but close my eyes and enjoy the feeling as convulsions of pleasure continued making James' hand soaking wet. By the time I was able to open my eyes again and relax my body, we were the only three people left in the dining area. Even with how amazing I had just been made to feel, I wasn't completely satisfied and ached for them to just take me right there and then. I was just about to slip under the table to try to take them in my mouth to ger them keener on the same idea (not that I doubted they were already) when the alarm started going off to let us know there was a dangerous event happening that needed us. Boss USA leapt up immediately, his rock hard dick still in my hand. He leant down, kissed my head and said. "We'll get back to this."

He tucked his dick away, which didn't do much to hide its firm bulge in his pants before he took off to be hero. Mike stood up too, lifted me up onto the table and bent down, kissed me on my clit through the hole in my pants before he stood back up and said. "What he said."

He took off too to be all heroic, leaving me having to dash to my quarters to quickly put a fresh supersuit on before I joined the fight.

Later, after another global threat had been dealt with, I needed to get cleaned up as well as destress so I drew myself a steaming hot bath with bottle of wine on bathside bench and soaked all the aches and pains of battle away while I day dreamed about the steamy events from earlier plus some extra happenings I wished had happened. A panel in the wall lit up showing that James was at my door. Excited, I let him know to come in and buzzed the door open, not that a closed or locked door could stop his super strong self. I heard his steps around the quarters looking for me so I called him into the bathroom. He stepped in, but quickly turned away because that's the type of good mannered guy he is. I laughed at him, told him it was okay, to come sit beside the tub and have a chat. Reluctantly he turned around. "Are you sure?"

"Don't tell me Boss USA is scared."

We both had a chuckle before he came and sat on the side of the tub. I leant my head on his leg. "Urgh, you're so lucky you got suped up. I'm so drained and sore."

The hinting worked as he placed his hands on my shoulders, began massaging me with strong grip. It excited me, knowing what he could do with his full strength and I was in those hands, yet he was able to do me just right with them, rubbing the tension out of me. Within minutes of the massage beginning, I felt him stroke my hair to the side before he began kissing my neck. Ohhh wow it felt good, his mouth on my flesh, the gentle biting between kisses had me forgetting all about the aches and pains in the rest of my body as my pussy heated up again. I moaned with pleasure as his mouth moved across my throat, arching my chest up as I pushed my neck deeper against his mouth. With eyes closed, I embraced how amazing it felt. Then one of his hands moved smoothly along my shoulder, down my chest to my breasts where he rolled one of my hard nipples between his fingers, sending pleasure chills through my body. His mouth left my neck before it moved to my other nipple, taking it into his mouth, teasing it with tongue and gently sucking it. Shit, I couldn't help myself anymore. I opened eyes, undid his pants and pulled out his half-engorged cock which was still more of a weapon at half mast than most men's. It was a daunting but impressive sight, especially so close to my face but I wanted it. With one hand one the side of the bath so I didn't slip and the other moving up and down his shaft with twisting motions, I blew hot breath on his massive knob to tease him a little, draw out the good feeling I was about to give him. My tongue licked up and down, around his knob, kissing the tip of it, faking taking it in for a few moments which made it grow so much bigger and harder, I could barely grip it. His hand ran through my hair as if he wanted to pull my mouth down onto him, as if he ached for it, yet didn't do it. So I rewarded him by sliding my lips, my mouth over his knob, taking the big rock and a little of his shaft into my mouth which brought a primal moan of pleasure out of him. I felt so powerful, making one of the strongest beings on earth moan with my mouth, him putty in my hands, at my whim and will. I couldn't take much of him in orally but I worked what I could with such a passion, combined with my fluid flicks or wrist while working the shaft, I soon ham him breathing really heavy, moaning and running his hands over my wet naked body, while he kissed my head. His fingers moving over my tender flesh got me even more worked up and I was soon using tongue over know and wet mouth over cock so passionately I was determined to make him explode. He might be one the strongest around but I had him in the palm of my hand, under my control, about to draw out such an exposed moment for anyone, let alone a suped up being. It was then that Mike's voice spoke through the wall panel as he knocked at my front door. With one eye I looked over to see his suave grin looking at the camera with a bottle of vodka in hand. This was it, I was finally going to get the dream fantasy. My mouth left James' cock to tell Mike to come in before I kissed James's knob once more and told him. "Take me to the bedroom and you'll get your reward."

He eagerly obliged, despite how close he had just been to cuming. His strong arms wrapped around me, lifted me out of the tub before he carried my wet body to the bedroom, holding me close against him. I kissed his neck on the way to keep his passion peaked before he laid me down on the bed. I took his cock I my hand again as I looked over at Mike and beckoned him in. He didn't need much invitation as the alcohol was tossed aside and clothes vanished into the tiny tech particles they were made of. As Mike was climbing onto the bed, James flipped me over onto my front and pulled my hips and ass up near him. The excitement and anticipation was almost too much as I knew that at any moment he would be entering me with his huge stonehard cock. I lunged my mouth at Mike's massive dick, vigorously sliding mouth up and down it while cradling his balls as I felt the tip of James' knob press against my soaked wet pussy entrance. I didn't know if he was going to be able to get much inside me, but I ached to find out just how much of his huge cock I could handle inside me. I could feel it pressing against me struggling to enter inside so I reach back and adjusted, helped guide it in. URGGGHHH FUUUCCKKK! I could feel every bit of it pushing against the insides of my pussy, putting pressure against all pleasure nerves, slowly filling up more and more of me as he pushed it slowly deeper inside. I almost choked on Mike's cock as I shrieked from James's moving further inside. "Oh fuck! Yes!"

Never before had I felt so completely filled. I went nuts on Mike's dick, slobbering all over his know and yanking with fast precision on his long shaft, using my tongue all of the edge of his know which made him pull my head down further, deeper around his cock. I fucking loved it, tried to take even more of it as James's started slowly thrusting back and forth, taking his know all the way back to the entrance of my pussy before shoving it back in deep which sent my mouth deeper down over Mike's cock. I was the pleasure center of it all, the spit roast, the one they needed to get their good feeling and the one making them feel good with my body while they made me feel even better. Before too long I found myself thrusting my ass backwards to meet the pumps of James' mighty dick, using the other end of the momentum to devour Mike's cock as deep as I could, taking his know down my throat, slurping up his shaft. Both powerful men moaned and groaned with primal noise as I used my mouth and pussy to take them both towards paradise at the same time. Two superheroes of the world, and I was the center of their worlds, taking them both on. Mike grabbed a handful of my hair as I sucked on one of his balls and frantically worked his cock with hand, making him groan out. "Oh shit!"

Every thrust between me and James brought us both closer and closer to orgasm, me especially as each time his cock went deep into me, stretched me out, I felt a bigger and bigger wave of joy growing down there, a red hot heat that was building up intensely inside me. Awww fuck, awwww fuck, I felt it getting closer. I wanted to get Mike off before me an James came so I took his whole cock deep into my throat and slid a finger up his ass which caused him to grip my head with both hands, hold it down in place as he spurted thick loads of cum into my mouth, again and again as his hands trembled on my head, his hips quivering and dick pulsating, emptying load that I swallowed all of. His grip on my head weakened as his body relaxed and I licked every bit of remaining sperm I could from around his knob, massaging it with my mouth to ease him out of the ejaculation moments with more pleasure. My focus was soon turned to what felt like growing waves of succulent warmth spreading out from my pussy, each bigger than the last as I neared orgasm, each powerful thrust from James taking me right to the brink of explosion, with any having the potential to be the one that sent me over the edge of joy. "Urrggh fuuccckk yes!"

My pussy exploded with feeling that swept through my whole body, suturing my mind in euphoria, clenching upon James' huge cock again and again, with powerful squirts in between that massaged and soaked his dick, causing him to let out such a groan of pleasure as he too unloaded deep inside of me. I could feel shot after shot of his hot cum hitting the end of my convulsing pussy as he held my hips tight back to him. Once I felt his body relax, I slowly pulled my pussy off his cock and got up on knees upright, kissed Mike on the mouth sweetly, running my hands through his hair, giving it a little yank as I winked. "Next time I'm facefucking you and you'll get this pussy."

We kissed sweetly for a few moments before I turned to James, kissed him and cleaned off the rest of our cum from his cock with my mouth before I laid down to rest, feeling completely satisfied, knowing I would get a great night's sleep, not caring if they stayed for the next round or not.

THE END

ilover 1 - BLOSSOM REBOOT

By the year 2100 Katherine had spent years stuck in the facility that kept her safe from the apocalyptic world outside. At least half of that time had been spent alone since the last of the other survivors died off. Before society had been wiped out, she'd been a brilliant scientist, at the leading edge of her field, even nominated for a nobel prize that she was robbed of when the world fell apart. For most of her years alone she'd been working on a project to that if successful, would make sure her sanity wouldn't begin to fall apart from isolation madness. There had been a few unsuccessful attempts along the way, as is the way with science, but like any good scientist knows, every failure is just another step towards the success. She ran over the diagnostics of the pulsanium body she had created and the A.I consciousness tech she had put into it. Once upon a time, the pulsanium she had used for the body (which she would call Steve) would have been worth billions of dollars, but that was when there was still a society to give it that value, now it was only worth what she was able to do with it. The years of setbacks and loneliness had her needing so badly for this to work. Sure she would keep pushing on and trying again and again if it didn't but damn she wanted it so badly. All the pre-tests came up positive and the moment arrived. She hit the button to activate the process that would hopefully bring the Steve to life and watched as the glow of power flowed through his body. Without realizing she was doing it, her breath was held in anticipation, eyes scanning for any movements, any signs of life, of success. Even with all the failed attempts, the excitement and hope still sparked bright in her every time she tried again and this attempt was no different. Her hands clenched together with peaked nerves as she waited and waited....

Nothing seemed to be happening though, which brought her energy crashing down as she slumped, accepting the fate of being alone for even longer. She stepped closer to Steve, stroked his face. "Someday."

Katherine leant down and pressed her lips to Steve's lips, gave him a sweet kiss before she stood back up to shut the process down. She got the shock of her life though when she looked over and seen his glowing penis was fully erect. "oh my ..."

As her pussy moistened on sight of the bright long cock, she looked back up and seen Steve open his eyes, reach his hand out to hold hers. "Kat?"

Her hand trembled in his as euphoria swept her. "Yes! I'm Katherine, I'm Kat. It's amazing to finally meet you, Steve."

His fingers caressed her hand as he sat up. "Katherine. Kat. The amazement is all mine."

Heart pumping, she moved closer, touched at his face. "How are you feeling?"

His hand glided up her arm with wide eyes, exploring touch for the first time, entranced by what Katherine felt like, the softness of her skin on his fingertips, the warmth emanating from her. "I'm wonderful, Kat. But you.. your arm, your body, it feels so.. so good. It's beautiful."

He gazed into her eyes. "Your beautiful."

Feeling almost breathless with excitement, Katherine moved closer, let his hands run over more of her body as hers moved over his. "Thank you, Steve. You're quite incredible yourself."

His hand ran gently through her hair, stroked softly against her face which brought a gentle sigh of enjoyment from her, caused her to move so close she could feel his dick pressing against her. Face to face, eyes locked onto each other, hands moving over each other's bodies, exploring, only a few millimeters remained between their faces. His hand placed on her back, pulled her the last tiny space remaining before they embraced in a kiss that was something neither had ever experienced before. Despite the strength of what Steve was made from, the kiss was soft, tender, caring and sweet as lips moved together with a slow passion that felt realer than life itself. His hand ran up and down the skin of her back as she fully embraced the moments, tongues softly dancing together in sweet formation as lips massaged against each other. His hands ran over her hips, traced down her legs and up her thighs which sent shivers through her, caused a little gasp that momentarily interrupted the kissing. Oral passion was soon returned to though as she pulled him up to be standing in her arms, his incredible penis pressed against her stomach as she pulled him closer against her body. This closer physical contact fired up the kissing speed a little as passion rose, yet warmth of caring remained. Katherine could feel herself moistening the longer it went on and moved one of her hands down to Steve's impressive dick, gently running her fingers along it, up and down it. She soon took it in the palm of her hand with continued movements up and down it which brought a gasp of pleasure from him that barely interrupted the dance of tongues and lips. Steve lifted Katherine up in his arms while still kissing and gently laid her down on the surface he had woken up on before laying down on the re too, beside her. Despite loving how it was all going, Katherine started to ache for more so she moved one of his hands to between her legs when she guided his movements to caress her clit how she liked until he was able to do it perfectly on his own. His fingers working with careful, but strong touch had her arching back as pleasure no one else had ever given her before ignited in her. She felt as if she was floating on clouds as his fingers massaged bursts of breathtaking pleasure in her which soon had her hand moving with increased passion along his cock. She wanted it in her so much, her pussy ached for it, yet what was already happening felt so beautiful, soul warming, she didn't want the greed for more to spoil it. If he made the move to enter her, she wouldn't resist, but she held back from being the one to make it happen. His mouth moved to her neck, kissing and sucking on her tender flesh while steadily working up pace and pleasure on her clit which had her slightly grinding hips up against the pressure of his hand. The sucking and kissing on her tender neck pushed her over the edge of desire. She slid her pants and underwear off and guided two of his fingers inside of her soaking pussy and pulled the palm of his hand firm against her clit to rub pressure against it as his fingers penetrated her. The kissing continued between them, even with the constant moans of pleasure that kept escaping Katherine from how good her made her feel. Breathing was heavy, as was heart beat rapid as he massaged surges of joy through her body, all the while was she was stroking his cock with firmer grip. A sensation grew quickly inside of her that was like nothing she'd ever felt before, yet it was like her body knew what was happening as pussy thrust hard against hand as it tensed up so tight before exploding in joy, gushing against his hand as breath deserted her in the midst of drowning in pleasure. Steve watched her expressions with intrigue, admiring every spasm and twitch, all the moments that showed joy. It was when she finally relaxed with deep satisfied smile that he kissed her forehead, whispered. "You're the epitome of beautiful."

Blushing, Katherine grinned and kissed him again. "I'm all you know."

Steve kissed her forehead. "You're all I want to know.. all I need to know."

If Katherine had ever felt happiness or content in her life before at any point, it was nothing compared to what she felt with Steve in those moments. She said. "I want you to make love to me."

His lips pressed against hers softly for a few moments. "I want to give you everything you desire."

Beaming with radiant glow, Katherine kissed him back. "Really?"

"Yes, sweet queen."

After having him do all her chores and tend to the vegetable gardens, Katherine led Steve into her bedroom. "Do you still want to give me everything I desire?"

Steve got down on one knee and lifted up the nightgown she'd put on. "For my entire existence."

He leant into her as she held his head while he kissed up her thighs, planting his mouth upon the edge of her pussy and stroking his tongue against her clit. Slow but powerful and consistent laps of tongue against her pleasure button soon had Kat moaning, rubbing her hands over his head and shoulders, massaging him as he rubbed her behind while making love to her pussy with his mouth. Katherine spoke to the base operating system. "Play romance list."

Music started playing from around the room as Steve penetrated Katherine's pussy with his tongue while pressing his thumb against her clit, gently rubbing it back and forth.

The music played a song from a long time before. 'now I want you so much.. the night is long.. and I need your touch. Don't know what to say.. never meant to feel this way.. don't want to be alone tonight. What can I say to make you mine.. falling so hard so fast this time.. what did I say, what did you do.. how did I fall in love with you.'

The feel those words with the music brought got Katherine pulling Steve up to standing before she led him to her bed. She laid down, guided him to be on top of her where she engaged in beautiful passionate kissing once more, except this time she had her heart set on far more. She stopped kissing and made sure they held strong eye contact when she asked. "Are you ready?"

Steve gave a reassuring nod. "As long as it's with you, I'm ready for anything."

Smiling, she began pressing their lips together again as she took his hard dick in her hands and guided it slowly and carefully into her pussy. He made no naïve attempt to thrust it in, only let her show it the way inside, each inch taking careful time until all of it was in her. The whole process brought many gasps and moans from Katherine who could barely contain herself from just driving it in deep. With eye contact held and sweet kisses given, her legs wrapped around him, pulled him in even deeper which made her cum right there and then. Whimpering with joy against his neck as her body shook with pleasure, she had to bite against him to contain from unleashing primal yelp of joy. When those initial convulsions settled down, she began kissing him again and gyrating her hips and pussy against him to move his cock out and in, shallow and deep, sliding along her pussy, pressing against all the sensitive places along the way. It didn't take long for him to get the feel of it and start to thrust his own hips slowly and patiently, lovingly pushing cock deeper into her before taking it all the way back to the edge and repeating the smooth motions again, each moment of those movements making Katherine feel even more amazing. Every bit of his cock pressing against the walls and depths of her pussy made her clinch him tighter to her, wanting more and more, deeper and deeper and her heart exploded with pure emotion and pussy blossomed in the midst of true connection pleasure. Steve kissed down her neck, her chest, slid the straps of her gown over her shoulders and kissed over her breasts as he made sweet love to her with determined but patient cock. The waves of pleasure kept increasing for Katherine as her pussy tingled and heated up more and more, made her wrap her legs around him tighter, pulled him in so deep she could feel his long dick pressing against the edge of her pussy every time he pushed inward. The feel of his mouth on her nipples had her grinding her pussy up against his thrusts in perfect passionate timing. Like a spark igniting, she started to feel that incredible explosion building up again as his mouth kissed and sucked and nibbled all over her breasts and nipples and neck. Gasping for breath in midst of joyful moans, she pulled his head into her neck while pushing pussy hard against thrust of cock. "ARRRUUUUGGGHGHH YES!"

Pussy clenched tight erupting on Steve's cock as Katherine spasmed beneath him, digging her fingernails into his back as she pulled him down closer to her. "Ohhh, I love you!"

Body trembled as pussy burst in such powerful pleasure, giving her goosebumps all over, muscles twitching while hotness and joy caressed body and mind. As she quivered in his grip, Steve stroked her gasping face with tender care. "I love you too, Katherine."

THE END

PIERCING 1

In one of the oldest houses in the New Orleans area, deep in the bayou, sat the vampire Adeve who was turned immortal at the age of 21 and centuries later glowed just as beautiful as ever. She had been alone for decades since the grandest love of her life (DRUSILLE) was emptied of her blood and burnt to ash. You might think with how quickly the years go by for a vampire that love and heartbreak would pass by easily but immortal creatures feel such things much deeper, more fiercely than humans because of all those extra years undead lovers are able to spend together. Now don't be fooled by the talk of Adeve's love, heartbreak and loneliness, don't let it lead you to think she's weak or any such thing. There was a time when her deeds spread fear like the plague in every corner of the world. She spilled more blood in violence than any war and that's not counting the blood she had to feed upon over her long, long life. That was when she was a young vampire though, before the rolling by of the years taught her patience and the value of traits greater than violence. She was still feared by a lot of the supernatural beings who had been around long enough to know what she was capable of, some of them even seeing it first hand, but it had been a long time since she unleashed her vicious wrath. Drusille had shown her things in the world, given her experiences, beautiful moments, opened her heart to the softer wonders of the world and changed Adeve's long life. Then she was taken from the world and a part of Adeve wanted to burn it all to the ground but she knew that would have broken Drusille's heart for Adeve to return to those ways so she kept herself busy with creativity, making music (which came easy as she had taught herself how to play almost every major instrument and allowed her to push al her pent up anger out through it) painting (which enabled her to express vivid emotion in images both disturbing and beautiful) and writing (which she used to pen her thoughts on the world, on society and humanity, on the wisdom she'd gained over her many years) Despite all that, all the distractions and coping methods, the loneliness remained and Adeve found herself seeking companionship. Things like dating apps made no sense to her who had come from a much older time so she began going out at night, bar hopping from place to the next as they all were incredibly unpleasant to her, that was, until she found a place where a young ebony woman (DELPHINE) sang with such deep emotion on stage, putting years of pain into her vocals which she sang so beautifully. Adeve found herself drawn in and by the time Delphine's set was done, Adeve was enchanted. She had to get to know this tortured young queen, hear all about the experiences that scarred her soul and see the pain in her eyes as she told the stories. The songs gave a taste and showed she had strength too, to put it out there for all to see but Adeve had never in her life been satisfied with just a taste. She went backstage to meet Delphine and could have used some of her supernatural power to put Delphine under a type of seduction spell but wanted to connect with her naturally and the mystic seduction ability took something away from who a person was. Adeve made it backstage to where Delphine was being harassed by a drunken bouncer who grabbed her arm. "Oh for f*cks sake Delphine, it's just a few drinks. I'm not asking you to marry me."

Delphine tried to pull her arm free. "Please just leave me alone, Steve. I'm not interested player, I've told you."

Steve snarled, his face ugly with nasty intent. "You dirty little c*cktease, you think you're better than me?"

Adeve moved across the room with supernatural speed and quietness and appeared beside Steve, broke his grip on Delphine and grabbed him by the throat. "When a queen like this woman speaks, you really should listen."

Steve choked and bashed at Adeve's arm to break free but couldn't budge her. He thrashed around violently to escape but was helpless. Adeve whispered in his ear with a little something extra in her voice. "On your knees and apologize."

Steve dropped to his knees, looked up at Delphine and begged for forgiveness. "I'm so sorry, please forgive me."

Delphine looked utterly shocked by it all but also relieved. "I.. You're.."

Adeve tossed Steve towards the door where he made a frantic scramble away. Adeve turned to face Delphine and made fierce eye contact while extending her hand as a greeting. "It's a pleasure to meet you, beautiful queen. My name is Adeve."

Delphine smiled with the warmth of a thousand good mornings and delicately shook Adeve's hand. "Delphine. Thank you so much for that. I was about to give him the old roundhouse kick to the face, so he was lucky you showed up, haha."

Adeve let a quiet chuckle slip out. "No doubt. I just wanted to come let you know how breathtaking your singing is. The raw emotion in the vocal, the pain in the lyric, it's.. it's.."

It had been decades since Adeve had found herself lost for words. Delphine helped her. "I understand.. thank you. You're very sweet."

They stood there for a few moments, simply gazing into each other's eyes, Delphine smiling her sunshine smile, Adeve feeling the energy, the soul of Delphine warming up her cold heart. She took a step back. "Well, it was an honor to meet you Delphine. I'll leave you to your business."

She turned to leave and got a few steps away when Delphine said "Keen for a drink or 3 with me?"

Adeve grinned and turned back around, forcing herself to subdue her smile before she did. "Okay, just don't take advantage of me if I find myself drunk."

Adeve couldn't get drunk, at least not on alcohol.. blood on the other hand gave her feelings similar to intoxication but different, more powerful, more primal. Delphine grabbed her bag and took Adeve by the hand. "You're safe with me."

"I feel it already."

They made a pitstop by the bar to order some drinks then nestled into a private booth in the corner of the club where they had some privacy but could still enjoy the live music. Delphine clinked glasses with Adeve and said "I was going to ask if you've been kicking it here long as I've never seen you round but your accent it pure New Orleans. Have you been away?"

Adeve thought quickly about all the years spent isolated from the world (except for when she had to feed) since Drusille's death then replied "My early years were spent abroad but then I ventured here with a great many people and this place became my home. It's been home, for so many very years now."

Adeve smiled as she drank. "You talk like you've got the years stacked but you look like you're barely old enough to drink.. except your eyes.. they look like you've seen the universe and experienced lifetimes of pain and pleasure."

Adeve didn't look away, only made stronger eye contact. "It surely feels like that in my heart. Life can become such a heavy thing, but it's times like this, meeting someone special like you that sparks the flame again."

Delphine chuckled, looked embarrassed and drank again. "You're so sweet, thank you."

"Welcome dear. So tell me, if you feel comfortable enough, it's quite alright if you don't, what is the inspiration behind your song Worthless? Who hurt you so badly and how?"

Delphine looked away for a few moments, gazing into her past, then looked back into Adeve's eyes, searching them to see if she could trust her with this painful truth. Adeve took her hand and rubbed it gently. "I understand if you don't want to."

Delphine took a deep breath. "It's okay. Back in the day, I was dating this guy, the first and last man I ever fell in love with and he was so sweet at the start, so loving and supportive of me and my music, then when we had been living together for a while, things started to turn. If I was late cooking him dinner because I got caught up in the flow of making a new song, he would lose his sh*t, shouting abuse at me and threatening to trash my instruments or throw me out on the street. For some dumb reason I let him convinced me I as in the wrong and a horrible girlfriend. Then he started getting paranoid and jealous about me performing here, at a bar, accusing me of sleeping with other men and stalking my every move. He guilted my ass into giving it up and being a good little stay at home wifey type for him, my world revolving around him while all I was was lost in it. My music is my power, who I am, my purpose and I was too afraid to even sing along to the radio anymore incase it sparked a rage fit in him. I did everything to be all he wanted and it still wasn't good enough for him. Every day of our lives together, he made me feel worthless and one day while he was at work, I started to write the song about it and doing that made me feel like my old happy self again and that's when I decided I was done with letting him ruin me, done with his rotten ass. I packed my stuff, left and crashed on a friends couch for a while until I had enough money saved to get my own little place."

"What happened with the ex? Do you still see him around town?"

Delphine shook her head with a greave look on face. "His next girlfriend had a lot of brothers who didn't appreciate the way he treated her and he went missing, hasn't been seen since."

"I'm so sorry you had to go through all that but so happy you found the strength to get out of it and find yourself again. This world would be a little colder without you and your music."

Delphine beamed warmth. "Thank you. You really feel my stuff, huh?"

"It's a beautiful experience to truly be able to feel the emotion, the love and pain of another through their creativity, their expression to the world. I don't know if any of my creative work has that power, as much as I try to make it so."

Delphine looked intrigued. "You're an artist? What do you do?"

Adeve sipped from her drink. "I paint, write, play some instruments, nothing with that magic you possess though."

Delphine grabbed Adeve's hand. "Will you show me? I would love to see your paintings, your writing, your music."

"Truly?"

Delphine put her empty glass down. "Hell yes! Let's go."

"Right now? You want to come to my home tonight?"

Delphine stood up with Adeve's hand still in hers. "Yes, if that's cool with you of course."

Adeve rose too, with cool elegance. "Yes, most definitely cool."

They caught an uber out to Adeve's home as she had flown into town and Delphine didn't own a car. Deep into the bayou they went, along roads that barely existed and past trees that were far older than the people passing them. The driver joked about it being kind of creepy and it did feel that way, even Delphine started to feel a little nervous until they pulled up in front of Adeve's mansion that stood out in the dark night like an old school glamorous beacon of classic style, rich with years of history. They paid the uber driver and got out of the car. Delphine stared in awe at the giant house. "Um, you didn't say you were rich. Damn!"

Adeve shrugged. "Money's easy to make with enough time. Come in, I'll show you around."

"Lead the way."

They went into Adeve's home where she showed Delphine all around the place, all through the rooms, the historic parts that remained unaltered, the expensive furniture, furnishings and art from around the world and time and finally into her creative room where many of her paintings hung. There was one on the easel that wasn't quite finished but Delphine found herself drawn right to it, past all the musical instruments. She stood in front of the unfinished painting, gazing in a near hypnotic stance at the image of a beautiful woman with a heartbroken expression, crying bloody tears as flames scorched the world around her, so vivid they seemed to almost be burning the very paper the paint was on. "Who is this? This tortured angel you paint? Is she a real person?"

Adeve stood by Delphine's side and gazed sadly at the painting. "Her name was Drusille. She was the love of my life for a long time until.."

Adeve kind of choked on her words, couldn't get the painful truth out without allowing tears to flow and she couldn't let Delphine see the tears of blood that would come out. Delphine put her arm around Adeve. "Something terrible happened to her, huh?"

Adeve simply nodded. Delphine asked "will you tell me about her?"

Adeve turned to Delphine and smiled. "Another time, if you're still interested. Tonight, I want to get to know you."

Delphine moved closer to Adeve, so close they could feel each other's breath on skin. Adeve could hear Delphine's heart racing in her chest although she could have heard that from a mile away as it was a part of her vampiric evolution to be able to detect such things. Delphine leaned in closer and planted a gentle kiss on Adeve's lips then pulled slightly back to study if she should continue. Adeve kissed her back and their mouths massaged with each other, slowly and tenderly. Delphine pulled Adeve's body tight against hers and traced her fingers over the back of her neck. Adeve kissed over Delphine's face, across her cheek and down her neck. She could feel Delphine's pulse beating with her lips and a younger vampire wouldn't have been able to resist the urge to sink fank into flesh right then but Adeve was older, wiser. She bit the inside of her own mouth to draw blood then kissed Delphine on the mouth again, spreading her vampiric blood in there to put Delphine in a kind of mystical haze so Adeve could taste of Delphine's blood and Delphine would think it all a drunken dream in the morning. It only took a few moments for the vampiric blood to make it into Delphine's system and the sign was she paused for a moment and moaned deeply before locking lips with Adeve again with charged vigor and intense feeling. They kissed with more passion than before, mouths smashing together as tongues swirled with each other, pressing and prodding while hands moved all over bodies. Delphine slid her hand down Adeve's pants and moved her fingers around her clit before pressing against it and rubbing back and forth over it. Adeve moaned in joy and placed her lips upon Delphine's soft neck, kissing, sucking and then swiftly bit down into a vein in her neck with her fangs. Delphine groaned in midst of erotic pleasure and worked even harder and faster on Adeve's pleasure button which in turn made Adeve want to suck her blood like a freshly turned vampire but she controled herself, her thirst and only gently drank a slight stream of blood from Delphine. She hasn't tasted anyone so delicious in a lifetime and it wasn't long before even the small amount of blood she drank made her feel that blood high, intoxicated off the life energy, whole body buzzing from it flowing fresh from her system. She felt as light as a cloud while at the same time kind of woozy but also crackling with electricity like energy. Delphine's fingers penetrated Adeve while thumb continued work on clit and Adeve had to stop feeding to catch her breath as she gasped and moaned, felt orgasm draw near. She returned to kissing Delphine's mouth as her whole body began to shudder as the orgasm swelled up inside her then erupted between her legs, drenching Delphine's fingers. Delphine put her fingers in her mouth and sucked on them seductively which drew Adeve even more wild, spurred her to pick Delphine up and lay her down on a couch where she ripped her pants off with sparked lust. Adeve drew blood from inside her mouth again and kissed Delphine, shared it with her to heighten her feeling of what she was about to do. Adeve kissed down Delphone's neck then moved to between her legs kissing over her clit, across her pussy and over her thigh. She sucked on her flesh there for a moment before sinking her teeth into her thigh while using fingers to flick across Delphine's clit. Delphine squealed out loud in ecstasy as her pussy got wetter, clit throbbed with pleasure and blood flowed into Adeve's mouth. She felt everything intensely as if her whole life had been lived with the dial turned down to minimum. Adeve drew her own blood again then moved her mouth to Delphine's pussy where she penetrated her with her tongue, probing with wicked skill, contorting it inside her like no mortal human could. As she massaged her clit, she curled her tongue up against her inner g spot, lapping against it with supernatural oral power, spreading her powerful blood into her pussy, rubbing it against the sensitive spots, heightening the whole experience for Delphine even more. It didn't take long before Delphine was arching her back, groaning loudly and pulling Adeve's head tight against her pussy as she felt the most tremendous orgasm build up inside her. One of her legs twitched out like crazy right before she exploded with brilliant pleasure, pussy clamping and seizing as Adeve kissed her clit, suckling upon it and teasing it with lips. Delphine let out a huge exhale of content and pulled Adeve up to be face to face. They embraced in a soft, caring kiss and Adeve laid down on the couch next to Delphine where they drifted off to sleep in each other's arms.

THE END

TILL THE FLAMES

Janika Monet sat at home alone on a Friday night, blazing a little green, well.. truth be told, a lot of green. It had been a mother*cker of a week at work in a job Janika felt sucking the light from her soul but it kept a roof over her head, food in her stomach and bills paid so she managed to tough it out, day by day, moment by moment. The green helped unwind, let go of all the stress and anger, push all that sh*t out before the next day of it building up again. Some of her friends were always on her back about 'Oh, you just need a man with a paycheck. He goes to work, you do what the f*ck you want all day and you just give him a lil something something to keep him happy' but Janika had yet to date a man she could bother f*cking with for longer than a few months. Most of the dudes she dated were either too street and unreliable or too nice and oh so boring and the rest wanted her to be their mother figure or sex slave. Now she could f*ck with the sex slave type long term if it worked both ways and there was any kind of deeper connection between them but the sh*t was usually fire for a short time before their personality made her very skin itch at their presence. She'd even been with a few dudes who struck hands on her and Janika liked to think of herself as a lady but she became something else when a dude had the damn nerve to strike her. You might think she maybe lost her sh*t and went crazy or waited patiently for the right moment to pay them back but what she did was much simpler. The last time a dude marked her up, she picked herself off the floor, started counting down from ten, walked calmly but determined to her handbag, pulled her gun out and aimed at the guy. The latest a guy ever called her bluff for was to the 2 count and the fire in Janika's eyes showed the dude he best get to rolling on as she re-aimed at his d*ck. Janika had given up on finding the right one and was damn happy doing what she wanted with all her free time. Yeah, she on occasion missed having a man to plow her down right with that primal energy but she had a couple of battery powered friends for that and she most definitely didn't miss dudes eating up all her food and smoking up all her green, nor did she miss the men who could afford their own sh*t but didn't get down n blaze with her or started talking bout gym gains when she wanted to get a good feed on. Janika shook her head at a dating ad on tv and went to sit out the back to get some fresh air and let her mind run free on bigger and better things as she gazed at the stars. The apartment building she lived in had a small courtyard out the back which a lot of the younger tenants would use for drinking or blazing but tonight it was completely free and quiet. Janika kicked back on one of the chairs, pressed the flame of her lighter to one end of a joint, inhaled deep, looked up at the stars and blew the smoke out at the ever expanding potential of it all above and around. Her chair wobbled a little and she planted her feet firm on the ground for balance but the tremors felt stronger there. Her first thought was of it being an earthquake but there were no car alarms going off around the neighborhood, nor dogs barking, nor people shouting, apart from the usual mother*ckers who always seemed to have something to shout about. The earth beneath Janika started to crack and break into pieces as smoke sifted out of it in hot puffs. Janika jumped back off the chair, kicking it away in her rush and backed up against the apartment building. "What the f*ck??!"

A smoldering hand clawed its way out of the dirt and grass and grabbed for leverage, gripped hard onto earth which sent Janika's heart beat pumping overtime as she fled back into her apartment for her gun. "Hell no!"

She snatched her gun out of her handbag and dropped it in the midst of her nerves. "God damn!"

She grabbed it back up and rushed back to the door looking out at the courtyard. She peered out the window and seen a man pulling himself up, bit by bit from out of the earth. His naked body was as dark as night and covered in scars that almost looked tattoos. Smoke rose from every inch of his muscular self as if he had just climbed out of the very flames of hell. Janika raised her hands and aimed the gun at the man whom roared as he pulled his body out of the earth. Flames licked up out of the ground the man rose from before he fully emerged and sat on hands and knees, sucking in deep breaths of fresh air. Janika steadied her trembling hand and kept the gun aimed at the man's head. His chest heaved and muscles bulged and tensed as he looked over to where Janika stood. Red flames flickered in his pupils and Janika felt her finger tighten on the gun trigger. The man raised a hand with palm up as if to say 'don't' and the flames vanished from his pupils to reveal an intense pain in his eyes that belied the ferocious energy the rest of him radiated. Janika could feel the pain in the man as their eyes locked in deep contact. She tucked the gun in the back of her pants, stepped closer to the man and extended a hand to help him up. The man hesitated and Janika almost spoke up to reassure him of his safety with her but he could see it in her eyes and he took her hand and rose to his feet, stood almost a full foot taller than Janika who felt goosebumps on her skin as she quickly looked over him from foot to face. He towered over her with impressive physical stature but she lead him inside with caring, soft touch. She looked around to see if anyone had seen them then closed the door behind them and led him into her living room. They stood staring at each other, still with hand in hand, eye contact locked, breathing in sync with each other. Janika dropped his hand and took a step back, overwhelmed by the crackling energy between them. She could feel greatness in him and herself as they gazed at each other, like she could feel that deep down potential inside herself climbing its way out of the depths, screaming to be unleashed, like he could do anything, achieve anything and so could she. He stepped closer to her and put his arm around her to kiss her which was rewarded with one of the quickest, snappiest slaps known to mankind, right across his face. Janika raised a finger. "That was first n last chance, mother*cker! Ima get you some clothes, aight. Just wait here."

The man gave Janika a small nod as a slight red mark appeared on his face from the slap. Janika stepped out of the room but peeked back around to see what the man did but his only action was to look around the room from his standing point. Janika knew there was some clothes leftover at the bottom of her closet from some of her exes that might fit this man so she went looking. She reentered the living room not long later with some baggy sweat pants and a large hoody. "That's all I got that'll fit you, brother."

She handed the clothes over. "Now you're going to tell me what the hell is up. I've known some wild dudes but never seen a mother*cker climb out of the earth with horns on his head, all smoldering n sh*t like his ass just crawled out of a fire."

The man slid the clothes over his body and they just barely fit. He stepped closer to Janika and finally spoke with a deep voice that commanded being heard and respected. "Where I came from, they called me Saleos."

"Okay Saleos, I'm Janika, but I ain'tcha n****r, yet. Now spill it, man. What are you?"

Saleos mouthed the name Janika before he replied. "You wouldn't believe it."

"I just seen you climb your ass out of the ground like some kind of zombie, didn't I? I think my mind is wide open right now!"

Saleos nodded. "You would call it hell. I called it home, for as long as my memories stretch back."

"You're a demon?"

Saleos nodded. 'I want something better though, something more than the pain around me down there, a reality greater than what those above manipulate to be. I want to make something better happen in this world."

Janika had dated some ambitious guys in her time. Some ended up in jail, some in the ground and one got too mother*cking big headed when the success rolled in and started playing like he was the king and Janika should be worshipping which did NOT go down well with her. She left his ass so quick, it took him a minute to remember she had dirty pictures of him and he offered her an insulting scrap of money to delete them all but she refused the money. Didn't need nothing from him but kept the pictures, just in case. She did still admire ambition though, when it was acted on. She had more respect for the people who hustled hard and ended up dead or in jail than she did for the dudes running their mouths bout what they gonna do who did nothing, played it safe. She seen Saleos literally pull himself up from the fires of hell to chase his ambition, so she had mad respect for him for that. She could see it in his eyes he meant what he said, that nothing and nobody was going to stop him, not even gods and devils. "So how you going to make that happen? You climbed your ass up here, what's the next step?"

"Learn how your world works, work it my way."

Janika nodded. "Cool cool, well I tell you what. We go at it together and split everything 50/50 and before you start thinking 'what can she possibly do to help me, a demon,' know this, I just clothed you, I got a couch right there for your ass to sleep on, if you sleep, I dunno, and I got food in the kitchen if you need to eat, so right now, I'm the one with all the mother*cking cards in the deck and ima hustle till the flames, man, so let's do great things."

Saleos grinned a little. "Till the flames. I like that."

Janika extended her fist to bump his. "We got a deal?"

Saleos held his fist out then bumped it against Janika's. 'Deal."

"Till the flames?"

He nodded. "Till the flames."

Janika strode off to the kitchen. "Good. Now come get some food. I'll heat you up some leftover chicken."

Saleos followed her into the kitchen. "Why are you helping me? I could feel you wanting to shoot me with your weapon when I rose up."

Janika pulled a plate out of the fridge. "Saleos.. man.. ima just call you Sales, aight. Hopefully that sh*t rub off on you cause as of right now, we a team and this food, the couch, it's an investment in the team. There's magic in you Sales, I can feel something great in you and I'd have to be some new level stupid not to roll with you on it, see what I can do with my potential before my ass turns grey n wrinkly."

Sales nodded. "Okay."

He took a piece of cold leftover chicken from the plate and devoured it. Janika was about to tell him off to wait till she heated it up, but he gave her the quickest of looks that closed her mouth real quick with the slightest tinge of fear in her. She let him go hard at the cold food, even munched on a couple of pieces herself. "Good huh?"

Sales grunted a 'mmhmm' as he ate. Janika handed him the empty plate. "We a team and I provided the food, so that makes you the washing up dude this time, my man, and don't be pulling that hellfire look at me like you did a minute ago cause I'll slap it right off your face."

Sales sat back and studied Janika intensely for a few moments with unbreaking eye contact before he got up and took the plate to the sink, started washing it. It wasn't long later that he entered the loungeroom and sat on the opposite end of the couch from Janika who was watching tv. "'I'm just catching the latest empire episode. You could learn a thing or two from sexy thang Lucious, that mother*cker runs sh*t and makes things happen."

Sales turned his attention from Janika to the television and watched the episode with her. Before too long, music started pumping loud from the apartment next to Janika's and drunken shouts could be hear with it. Janika got up aggressively and banged on the wall. "Ey! Keep it down man, empire is on!"

A voice shouted back at her. "F*ck off b*tch!"

Janika inhaled a deep breath and marched out of her apartment. "Ohh, no you didn't just call me a b*tch!"

She entered the hallway and went to the front door of the next apartment and banged on it. A huge guy with prison tatts all over him answered the door which let the loud music spill out more as heaps of other people partied inside. "What?!"

Janika looked shocked. "What? What?! First of all, which one of you dirty bastards called me a bitch? And second, you're.."

The huge guy pushed Janika away from the door. "Hoe."

Janika stumbled backwards, almost fell over but scrambled back quick. "Motherf*cker!"

She sent a straight right jab true into the guy's nose which instantly bled. "Who's the hoe now?!"

The other people partying cheered and gasped, went wild. The huge guy growled and swung a fist as hard as he could at Janika's head…

But that giant menacing fist was caught inches from Janika's face by Sales who snapped the guy's wrist backwards, broke it. The guy screamed out in pain and tried to swing his other fist at Sales who repeated the process on that hand too. The guy staggered backwards staring at his floppy wrists with fear in eyes. Sales followed him with clenched fists and a low primal growl coming from chest. Most of the partying people started freaking out and some got aggressive and moved on Sales who swatted their drunken attacks away like they were flies who got sent crashing through furniture. A loud shout rang out and Sales turned to see a guy with a gun aimed at him. Sales growled and advanced on the armed person who fired without hesitation. The bullet just missed Sales and struck the wall behind Janika, right next to her head. Sales looked back, seen how close it had gotten to Janika and stepped in between the line of her and the gun. Another shot fired and struck Sales right in the chest. He stopped his forward movement to touch the wound before he advanced again with double the pace and a look of primal anger on his face that would scare a pack of lions away. The gunmen stepped back in fear to give himself time to aim a shot at Sales head but tripped on someone else's feet and lost his balance. Sales was on and snatched the gun out of his hand before another shot could be fired.

Sales held the gun and shoved the firing end into the guy's mouth, ready to blow his head off when Janika screamed out. "Stop!"

She rushed to his side, took the gun from his hand, wiped it clean of prints in her shirt and let it drop to the floor. The original shooter stared in shock and fear at the bullet hole in Sale's chest. "You should be dead, man."

Sales leaned in close and whispered in his ear. "So should you, if it wasn't for her good heart. Keep the music down."

"Yeah man, of course, no sweat, I got you."

Sales let go of the man's throat and strode calmly out of the apartment with Janika in front of him. The music was quickly turned down behind them as they got back to Janika's apartment. Sales sat back down on the couch, right where he had been sitting before. Janika stared at him. "You a bad mother*cker huh?"

Sales turned his head to face her. "Had to be. Came from hell, remember?"

Janika glanced at where the bullet struck Sales. "True. So are you like invincible or some sh*t?"

Sales undid the hoody he was wearing and somehow used his body to force the bullet out of him which dropped to the floor. "Not invincible, just hard to kill."

Janika admired Sale's rippling six pack and defined muscles and even if she wouldn't admit it, she found herself aroused by the sheer powerful force Sales had shown in having her back. Plenty of dudes had mouthed off for her, even traded blows with other dudes but this guy just took a bullet for her and intimidated a whole room of bad dudes into 'bowing down.' She sat beside him on the couch and touched the bullet hole, let her hand slide down over his chest and stomach. "You want a bandage for that?"

Sales shook his head and gazed deep into Janika's eyes which sparked her even more. She moved her hand down further and stroked it over the hard bulge in Sale's pants before she leant in closer and pressed her mouth to his in passionate embrace. He returned the passion with extra and grabbed her with raw strength, sat her down facing him on his lap where she grinded her warming self against his giant manhood. Her hands explored his firm body traced over his muscles as he kissed and bit softly against her neck before he ripped her top off with one hand and moved his mouth to her chest where he sucked and teased. She gyrated her hips against his hardness with more passion and lust as both of their breathing got deeper and heavier. His strong, rough hands explored her body, sending electricity like sensations through her before she undid his pants and slid her hand inside. He threw her off him and down onto the couch, knelt over her and tore her pants off before positioning himself between her legs. She slapped him, embraced him in more heavy kissing and pulled his rock hardness out which made her hand feel so tiny holding what felt like such great power. He grabbed her hands and held them in one of his above her head as he entered her welcoming self with all of his rock hard power. Janika yelped in pleasure and pain as she felt filled like no mortal man had ever been able to accomplish. She gasped for breath as Sale's powerful thrusts rocked her whole body and soul, deeply. She quickly adjusted to the new level of sensations she had never experienced and began to buck against Sale's thrust, their pleasure colliding in explosive combination. Janika's whole body seized up and shuddered as she exploded in otherworldly joy. Sales leant down, kissed her then flipped her around onto her knees and elbows and drove in again from behind with movement so strong Janika's face planted deep into the couch cushion as she wailed shrieks of pleasure and arched her back low. Sales pushed in deep and hard, again and again and Janika felt her whole body start to convulse as she erupted again, which in turn brought Sales to mighty explosion inside of her. Janika turned around to be laying on her back as she panted heavily, recovering form the incredible experience. She stared at Sales who returned the gaze as both caught their breath. "How you going to f*ck like that on your first day on earth, damn!"

Sales grinned. "Primal instinct or some sh*t like that."

Janika smiled. "Your ass still sleeping on this couch though."

"Cool."

Janika got up and grabbed a sheet and pillow from a drawer, tossed them to Sales. "That's you. Ima chase some z's."

Sales caught the sheet and pillow, gave Janika a slight nod before she went to her bedroom.

The next day Janika awoke to the enticing smell of eggs cooking in her apartment. She groggily got out of bed, tossed a robe on and went out to the kitchen where she seen Sales adding some seasoning to some scrambled eggs he was cooking. He seen Janika and gave her a wink as he pulled some toast from the toaster and tipped the eggs onto it, on a plate and handed it to Janika. "Day 1. Feed up n let's get this world."

Janika enjoyed a mouthful off the best scrambled eggs she had ever had. "Aight Sales, damn. All ready to hustle n sh*t. I got our day 1 goal for you."

"Speak it."

Janika swallowed another tasty mouthful as she tapped her fork against the plate. "I know this RnB/hip hop duo 'Soul Shine' who are fire in human form. He sings like a ghetto angel and she raps like a poet from hell and together they flow like.. like.."

Sales spoke. "The forces of nature combined"

"Yeah, something like that. So, despite their obvious fire, they ain't getting no radio play or any decent promotion to get their flame out there and it's because they signed with the first shady mother*ckers to offer them representation who won't let em free from the chains."

Sales made a gun trigger motion with his fingers and raised his eyebrows a little as if asking a question. Janika shook her head. "Nah, but we're going to find some way to free em then get em signed up with us, see, I started my own lil management company because artist rep is where some big money is at and the duo I'm talking bout is going to be the act that makes my name, our name. Just got to free em up."

Sales rubbed his chin. "N how does that make something better happen in this world? Something truly great?"

Janika swallowed another mouthful and pushed the empty plate over to Sales. "Wait till you hear them perform. You'll see."

Sales pushed the plate back over to Janika. "I cooked, you clean."

Janika aimed a fierce, unblinking stare at Sales n bit her lip. Sales returned the gaze with a flicker of fire in his eyes which brought an amused chuckle from Janika. "Fair enough, man. You lucky the feed was good."

After they got done at home, Janika took Sales to a nearby thrift shop to get him some threads to wear. "Can't have you looking like a street dude when we trying to hustle to higher levels. Keep that bad demon gaze ready in your pocket though."

Sales stood tall in a dark, pinstripe suit Janika found and checked himself out in a mirror. Janika looked him up and down, felt her heart beat race a little. She thought he looked finer than heavenly wine and more dangerous sexy than any Denzel or Michael B Jordan character. "Yeah, that'll do, you got it."

She held up a tie to his chest before tossing it back on the rack. "F*ck a tie. Unbutton them top two button as well. Yeah that's it. Now you look like a mother*cker who knows his business but can win getting dirty too. Hurds ain't going to know how to come at you."

Sales adjusted his collar a little. "Hurds?"

"Yeah, hurds, hurdles, tricks, marks, wannabe hustlers, b*tches, dude or chick, don't matter. Anyone who's in between us and our goals is a hurd and we have to leave them all in our wake."

Sales brushed a piece of fluff off his jacket sleeve. "We got this."

"Cool. Now, I've hit up Soul Shine to organize a meeting with their joke ass label and we're going to ambush them greasy mother*ckers and get them to release the duo so we can sign them and get to work on blowing them up, setting fire to the charts and building the base of our kingdom."

"So you want me to rough some mother*ckers up so they sign a release or some sh*t?"

"Hopefully it aint come to that and you just be there, looking all demon fury power an that's enough but be ready for whatever, improvise, whatever it takes, we're going to make it happen. Just don't kill nobody."

Sales nodded. "Cool."

They met up with Soul Shine out the front of a piece of sh*t building that was full of rinky dink ass businesses on every floor. Soul Shine, which was made up of Cedrice the sister and poetic genius who spit truth fire and Jerone the brother who sang so god man smooth and beautiful women and men would throw their hearts with their panties at him when he sung. Cedrice embraced Janika. "Hey buu, I feel it in you today, I do. We're not only gon break these chains that hold our souls to the ground but set fire to the oppressor's evil."

Janika hugged her back. "Oh we got you, that's the truth. It's good to see you, love, and it's going to be even better showing these mother*ckers what's up."

While they were talking, Jerone offered a fist to bump to Sales. "Hey, my brother, thanks for coming to aid our journey."

Sales gave him the fist bump. "Respect. Janika says you're something higher level, something that can touch the hearts, souls and minds. I'm about that energy."

Jerone smiled warmly. "Much love brother."

Sales gave him a slight nod. Janika flung her arms around Jerone. "My brother, you ready to soar like a mother*cking eagle?"

"My sister, it's been a minute since our energies flowed together but I'm feeling so good, I can feel the wings on my soul and they've been itching, they've been scratching, they're ready."

Cedrice gave a head raise nod to Sales. "What's up brother?"

Sales glanced up at the sky. "Glowing angels with no heart and gods so far."

Cedrice looked impressed. "I feel that my poetic brethren. You sound ready to tear them all down in blood and flame and help lift us, let us down here in the grime and crime rise again."

Sales liked not only the words that came out of Cedrice's mouth but the energy of them, how she made them sound, the power of the meaning in them. He knew right there and then that if she could touch him with her words that easily, she could inspire great change if given the right stage. Her and her brother who radiated powerful good energy and love. Janika caught the way Sales looked at Cedrice and didn't like how it sparked a flicker of jealousy in her. She brushed it off and focused on the mission. "Right, let's get this."

They entered the building which had an out of order elevator, so they took the stairs up to the floor the so called record label had its office on. The office had two small rooms of which one was the entrance where a pimply youth (Justin) who barely looked out of high school age sat at a little table with a scratched up laptop on it. Justin was the nephew of one of the two guys who ran the label and worked for them for less than minimum wage. His look of excitement at seeing Soul Shine quickly turned to fear as Sales and Janika followed them in. Now, you can put it down to Sales being a fearsome looking dude or the fact that Justin wasn't used to being alone in a room with a group of black people, but he stammered and scurried to open the door to the other room for them, right quick. "Th.. th.. this way, if you want, they're waiting for you, I mean, not that you're late, just they're.."

Jerone placed a gentle hand on the young man's shoulder to calm him. "Thank you. Much appreciated young breeze."

Justin smiled awkwardly and held the door open for them as the four entered the other room where the two owners of the label sat. One (Tony), sat behind a desk and the other (Ben), sat on a chair next to a couch. Tony dressed in a cheap suit with slicked back hair greeted them with the false smile of a snake while Ben, dressed in work pants and a plain jumper, with unkept hair, offered hand shakes without getting out of his chair. There were only 3 available seats on the couch which Janika, Jerone and Cedrice sat in after Sales took a stand right next to Ben where he towered over him, made him look up and around nervously. Tony banged his hand against his desk enthusiastically. "Soul Shine, Soul Shine, what can we do for you and your fine looking friends today?"

As he was saying that, he opened a secret slot in his desk with his leg which no one noticed him do except Sales who stared unblinking at him. Janika took a release form out of her jacket and handed it over to Ben who had started leaning forward in his chair because of his discomfort at Sales standing over him. Ben studied the form for a moment before screwing up his face and handing it over to Tony. Ben shook his head and scowled at Janika but he switched his gaze to the floor when Sales started tapping his fingers against the back of Ben's chair. Tony reached into his secret drawer as he pretended to be studying the paperwork after he already seen what it was but by the time he had pulled his pistol out, Sales had moved to right behind him and placed, with firm grip, one hand on the back of Tony's neck and another on the shoulder of the arm that held the gun, stopping him from being able to lift it to use it. Tony tried to sound big despite the fear across his face. "What the f*ck is this?!"

Cedrice and Jerone looked as nervous as a woman around the POTUS T. Cedrice went to get up. "This isn't how we roll, L."

Janika put a hand on her knee. "It's okay, trust me."

Tony screamed. "Justin! Call the police n tell them we're being robbed by gangbangers! Now!"

Justin peeked around the door and seen the situation, seen the gun in his uncle's hand and knew from his time working there how many artists the label ripped off. Justin was actually a huge fan of Soul Shine's music and had played their demo so much he could recite all the lyrics off by heart. Now, Justin also knew he would catch such a whooping from his whole family if he didn't do right by them and make the call to the police and he was about to go do so when Jerone gave him a look and a slight shake of head and mouthed the words 'please don't.'

Ben screamed at him. "Call the damn cops, Justin!"

Everyone in the room stared at him to see what he would do and he felt his heart race and the world started to spin. His legs gave out beneath him as he passed out from overload of nerves and crumpled to the floor where his head would have crashed hard if Janika hadn't caught it at the last moment. "Easy, white boy. Noone's dying here today."

Ben seized the chance while others were distracted to grab a baseball bat from behind his chair and lunge towards Sales, swung the bat as hard as he could at his head. Cedrice screamed out "look out!"

Sales was well aware of the coming attack though as his demonic senses were far superior to those of an out of shape, middle aged, alcoholic human. Sales pushed down harder on Tony's shoulder, forced his face against the desk and with his other hand, grabbed the bat clean in midair with little trouble. He yanked the bat and Ben towards him, dropped the bat and grabbed Ben by the throat. "Sign it."

Ben and Tony both squirmed and flailed but couldn't break free. "Screw you man!"

Sales pulled Ben's face real close to his and fired up the demonic flame in his own eyes which made Ben's blood feel cold and laced with the fears of every dark moment he'd ever had. "Sign it."

"Okay, okay, damn!"

Tony shouted. "Don't you f*cking sign that, I swear to god!"

Sales tossed Ben at Janika's feet, knowing full well he wouldn't try anything sneaky now he'd copped the flowing fear stare. Sales then squeezed Tony's shoulder to make him drop the gun and pulled his face up real close to his and gave the flowing fear stare again. "God doesn't care!"

Tony's blood felt like ice as he trembled in Sale's grip. "I'll sign, I'll sign."

Tony dropped to the floor beside Ben and added his signature to the release form Ben had already signed. Janika snatched up the form. "Pleasure doing business with you slimeballs."

She held her hand up for Soul Shine to leave the label's office. "Time for a new chapter, my loves. Let's get ours."

Cedrice and Jerone left the office but Janika and Sales lingered, gazing at each other over the people on the floor. Outside the office, Jerone whispered to Cedrice "That was some heavy, neg energy stuff in there. Are we sure we want to let them rep us?"

Cedrice took her brother's hand. "We know Janika, that she loves our music in her heart and soul, that she believes in it and us. Yeah the big man can flow with the hellfire but he's on our side, doing it for us. I'd say they make a pretty damn good representation team, especially compared to those last slithering scavengers."

Jerone smiled with a nod. "There's something fierce about them together isn't there?"

Janika spoke as she was followed by Sales out of the office. "Fierce, formidable, ferocious. We got you, fam."

Janika exchanged the bumping of fists on top of fists with Cedrice and Jerone and Sales copied the motion followed by a firm handshake with Jerone that included deep but good energy eye contact. "I got you, man. If your music can spark change, I got you till the flames."

Jerone grinned. "Okay than, brother. Let's make magic happen."

Cedrice bumped fists with Sales and said "till the flames."

Janika threw her arm around Jerone and both said "till the flames."

A unity had been formed, a connection with such fierce loyalty in pursuit of dream that no mortal should dare attack it. The group found themselves at Janika's apartment, celebrating the new stage of life with bottles of Hennessey and Vodka. It didn't take many drinks for Cedrice to rip out some rhymes as the others admired. "I done come into this world where my energy devalued, I tell you right now that I won't be bowing, hell no. Can I get a hell no?"

(The other three shout "hell no!")

"Hell no said the man when they looking down upon me, but I turn the chains to ash, phoenix getting angry, blame me for your prejudice and I don't even know you, hate me for my sur viv al an ima climb above you!"

Jerone jumped in with some sweet vocals. "Ohhhhh up, up, up. Weee, don't stop, stop, stop. I got love for my brothers and sisters.. I see the heart in yaaa.. Such a powerful force we be holding in our souls. Such a beautiful spirit, we on ours, not their goals. We're the super soaring phoenix who gon crawl out of the bed they made. Metaphysical brilliance that'll lift us past the hate."

Everyone there could feel the intense power and heart that radiated from them when they did their thing, especially Sales who felt Jerone's vocals on a whole different level than the others as he had dug himself out of hell to escape the hate, the negative energy, the preconceptions of what he should be and sought something greater in the mortal world, something new level, something so jarring to the preconceived notions of how things should be, it's influence reached heaven and hell. This music, this emotion, the depth of truth and pain and love sparked something in him his soul had been aching for. Jerone noticed how deeply Sales got into it and passed him an imaginary mic. Show us what your heart speaks, brother. I can see you got stories on stories."

Sales stared at Jerone for a moment before he leant forward and started. "Yeah I got stories upon stories, million tortures chasing glories, I got scars that mark my very bones, soul wounds that keep on pouring, but I never gave a tear to life, I come from demons gnawing."

Sales leant back in the chair and drank some Hennessey. Jerone nodded and smiled, impressed. "Truth flows with scarred wings out of pain and is so beautiful."

Cedrice bumped her fist against her chest. "Pure, brother, pure."

Janika ran her hand over Sales leg as she leant forward to get another drink but the bottle was out of reach. Sales reached out with his long arm span and grabbed the bottle for her, poured some more in her glass. Janika gave him a wink before she raised her glass in the air between them all. "To Soul Shine and Till the flames management!"

They all clinked their glasses together which gave off an almost cracking clink. "To Soul Shine and Till the flames!"

Soul Shine lasted a few more hours before they caught an uber home at which point Janika and Sales damn near broke each other in their alcohol numbed f*cking that had even some angry kept awake neighbors jealous as hell and intrigued by the primal shrieks and roars of pleasure. Sunrise met the passion before Janika collapsed, unable to keep going. She panted and sweated and pulled Sales down next to her on the floor, wrapped his arm around her. "Need sleep. Gotta work on Soul Shine exposure today."

Even the demonic power enhanced Sales needed to catch his breath and felt a bit worn as Janika laid her head on his chest and he wrapped his mighty arms around her glistening, beautiful, black body. "Rest well, sweet queen."

They only got but a few hours sleep before Janika's dry mouth, spinning head and aching body broke her slumber in Sale's arms. She lurched up and made a stumbling dash to the kitchen sink where she unleashed the faucet's full power and guzzled cool, healing water. She drank and drank until it felt like she might vomit it all back up. She stood there, leaning against the sink, eyes closed, head spinning and heard Sale's footsteps behind her. She grabbed a nearby clean glass, filled it with cold water and thrust it out in the direction of Sales who took it and quenched his own thirst with a mouthful which was a lot for him considering all the years he'd spent in the dry fires of hell, adapting to those conditions. He put the glass down. "You good?"

Janika waggled her finger a little. "Uh uh. Hell no. I need two bacon n egg rolls, stat! There's money in my purse. Bakery."

"Aight, I'll be back soon."

Janika gave a poor attempt at a wave. "Good. Then we get to work."

She dry reached and turned the water on again. "Hopefully."

Sales moved with surprising pace with his long strong legs and made it to the bakery and back in little time. When he did get back, Janika had moved to sitting at the kitchen table with her head on arms against it and a jug of water close by. Sales tossed the food on the table and Janika snatched it up real quick. "Grease! Yes!"

She devoured one fo the bacon and egg rolls like a starved lion upon finally finding prey, and washed it down with more water, then rested her head in hands again. "Right, how do we make Soul Shine catch fire? How do we.. How do we quickly get them the exposure they deserve?"

Sales had been thinking on it as he was on the food run. When he noticed that a newsstand was getting business from being in front of a popular bakery, it started giving him ideas and the first one he spoke of was. "What if we take them to the outside of all the major record labels, at times when the high up, powerful people there are arriving or leaving and have them perform the hottest track right where the powers that be can't help but hear it? That could lure in a dope deal with legit people damn quick."

Janika gazed over at him. "Okay, that could be fire but those places probs already have heaps of other unsigned artists trying the same thing."

"But are they Soul Shine?"

Janika slowly shook her head. "Uh uh."

"And do they have the universal, powered up, soul flow that Soul Shine does?"

"Hell no!"

"And do they have the metaphysical, might of poetic truth that Soul Shine does?"

"Nah uh."

"So f*ck what others can't do, cause we know Soul Shine got that extra extra to do what 'can't be done,' right?"

Janika slapped her hand against the table. "Motherf*cking right!"

She winced and held her head, drank some more water. "I hope you know how to drive cause I ain't fit for that sh*t right now and I'm not messing around with all that public transport noise today."

Sales took a bite of one of the egg and bacons rolls and pushed another into his partner's hands. "I got you."

She held eye contact with him that coincided with her heart feeling some kind of warm and fuzzy. "You really do, huh?"

He felt home in her eyes, in her presence and it disturbed him in a way that someone who grew up on Antarctica might feel if they moved to an Australian summer. She placed her hand on tops of his which caused him to pull away. "Ima jump in the shower real quick, get the smell of liquor off me before we go trying to secure record deals."

Janika felt hurt for a moment at Sales pulling away but she had seen the ways he looked at her, in her eyes, the things he did for her, the powerful energy between them. She knew there was something there, some feeling between them and she had no doubt the dude would be freaking on it after growing up in hell. Sh*t, many mortal dudes freak out more over less. Janika had been around long enough to know to play it cool and not scare a mutherf*cker off. She also knew she wanted him as her king and to bless him by being his queen. "Cool, I'll jump in after you."

Sales gave a slight nod of head before he vanished into the other room, his mind a mess on what was going on in his heart. Janika smashed down some more food into her stomach and rose to her feet. She heard the shower start running and slipped off her clothes as she made her way into the bathroom. Sales was in the shower, the water glistening over his sexy, muscular, darkness. It felt so good over his body, so refreshing and cleansing, he ached for Janika to be in there with him and that's when she appeared, her breathtaking, ebony, nakedness on full display for him as she entered the shower too. His eyes couldn't help but scan her naked body, the beautiful dark skin, the curves, the scars, the extra erotic delights and before he knew it, she was lathering up his body with a soapy wash cloth which slowly (but not too slowly) worked its way from the back of his neck, down to his suddenly rock hard manhood. She got down on her knees to 'clean' him properly and made him feel like heaven was right there, like all of his strength was nothing compared to her oral power. He felt helpless and like a king at the same time. He raised her up when it was done, kissed her and turned her around. She began to protest that her body couldn't handle more of that today when she realized he was gently washing her, taking care to attend to every inch of her body. She smiled and closed her eyes, enjoyed the hot spray of water against her naked skin as her lover's firm but tender touch took care of her. He turned her around again to face him which made her open her eyes. She touched her hand to a scar on his neck and leant in and kissed it softly. Her mouth moved up to his which led to a sweet embrace as their lips pressed against each other, tongues met in middle. There was a feeling erupting between them that many would use words to try to express but their touch, their eye contact said more than enough between them. She said "ready to take the world."

He responded "with you? Always."

A few hours later they arrived, with Soul Shine, at the first of the big record labels on their list. Cedrice, gazed up at the offices. "Y'all 100 on this, fam?"

Janika led them to the part of the parking lot where the best and most expensive cars were parked. "Yup. All we got to do is wait for one of these super high up mother*ckers to come out to their car and hook em with your magic."

"Aight, you're the management."

It wasn't too long before one of the well known high ups came striding out towards their car with two assistants scurrying right behind. Sales gave Jerone a gentle slap on the arm. Jerone nodded and glanced at Cedrice who winked at him. "Let's get this."

Jerone started serenading with the smoothest, sweetest harmony as Cedrice unleashed a verse of pure poetic, truth fire that would have had Tupac on his ass. Their target barely even glanced at them and rolled his eyes. Jerone stepped up with a beautiful vocal that Mariah Carey couldn't touch but their target just shook his head and got in his car. He drove away as Soul Shine stood there, speechless. Janika gave the car the bird. "What the f*ck was wrong with him? You were fire and sugar, like, f*ck!"

Soul Shine looked discouraged with slightly negative body language. Sales stood in front of them with impressive confidence. "If you're building your house, your empire and you miss when hitting the first nail, are you going to give up on the whole house? Hell no. You keep banging away till you 've got what you want. Sh*t don't come easy or quick."

Jerone rubbed his nose. "Truth, truth."

The next high up person that came out got such a brilliant performance but offered nothing but a nod of head. Soon Janika and Sales were quick and preaching fire game to go with the incredible vocals of Soul Shine but no luck was had. The day wore on into night as they tried different labels across the city and tempers rose as the heat of the day mixed with the rejections got to them. Cedrice muttered in the back seat of the car "got us out here like slaves, singing for the white man, some bullsh*t!"

Janika almost swung around and snapped back but Sales grabbed her hand and shot her a look to cut that out real quick. Janika took a deep breath. "I know it feels sh*t but this is the grind, the hustle, feel? Winning don't come easy and one success is built on a thousand failures. Just got to keep.."

Cedrice interrupted, her hurt pride radiating loud. "Enough! Our throats are wounded and souls beaten down. We done with this disrespect and humiliation."

Janika swung around. "You quitting?"

Jerone waved that away. "Nah, nah, our dreams can't be quit on. We just need a new idea, new approach to it."

Cedrice added "and some damn food and sleep… on our own."

Sales grunted. "We'll drop you off at ya crib, than, get back to you tomorrow with a better idea."

Cedrice. "Mmhmm."

They drove in tense silence till they reached where Soul Shine lived. Jerone touched Sales and Janika on the shoulders before he got out of the car. "I know your eyes and fists be having our backs n wings, it's just been a day with dragging time."

Cedrice waited until Jerone got out and leaned closer to Sales and Janika. "My blood out there is too gentle to flow with it so I have to be the trigger for him but if you grind our hearts through another day like the one just rolled out, we might need to spin the management cycle again."

Before Janika could clap back, Cedrice was out of the car and following Jerone into their apartment building. Janika shook her head and sat in silence the rest of the drive home, just staring out the window and tapping her fingers against the door. They finally made it home without a word spoken and when they got inside, Sales moved to kiss her and give her the D to unwind some of the stress but Janika pushed him away with hard hands on chest. "For real, mother*cker?! I knew it was a stupid god damn idea to have em out there like that but you and your sword from hell had me tripping, thinking you some kind of genius maybe. Stupid ass fool!"

Sales bit his lip to try and stop himself but he wasn't going to let this mortal talk down to him like that and his pride got the best of him. "B*tch, what?! I didn't hear ideas flowing from your mouth that never seems to shut up!"

Janika clenched a fist in one hand and pressed a finger into Sales chest with the other. "Who the f*ck you think you are, talking to me like that? In my home?! You think you scare me?! I ain't scared of you, mother*cker!"

Sales blew out a sharp burst of 'not caring' air. "Pfft! Pathetic mortal!"

Janika's eye lit up and she hit Sales with a jab so quick to the cheek bone, even he was caught off guard by it. Janika got up on her toes and stared him right in his face. "What?! Huh? What now?!"

Sales tried to wrap his arms around her to calm her down but she struck him again and again for each time to tried to hold her to subdue her. His face took an absolute pummeling before Janika collapsed against him, exhausted, her head resting against his firm chest. She tried to push him away again but he held her tight to him in his strong arms as she said "how she going to talk to me like that after all I'm trying to do for her. Everybody always disrespecting when I give my energy to their life, like wtf?"

Sales kissed her head, his pride and heart weakened by her emotional vulnerability. "You deserve better, buu. She'll realize she was tripping."

Her lifted her up and carried her to the bedroom where he laid her gently down on the bed and kissed down her body, slid off her pants and underwear with his teeth. He stayed down there and took care of her so well for so long that she (later on) got the best night sleep she'd had in a very long time. She awoke the next morning feeling so refreshed and worlds better, excited to make goals happen and heal relationship/friendship wounds. She smiled as she remembered how her man worked out all her stresses the night before and went in search of him to find him on youtube on her laptop in the kitchen with a pot of coffee next to him and a heap of scribbled notes. "Morning stud. Been hard at it, I see."

Sales looked over at her with excitement and took her hand in his. "I got it this time, I know it, well if you feel it too, anyway."

"What's that? Whatchu got for me?"

He winked at her. "Oh I got something for you but that can wait till later. Check this."

He switched to one of the many internet tabs he had open and showed her a promotions page on youtube with audience targeting specifics like taste in music, age, gender, location plus prices for boosting a promotion and set time lines for the promo. "Now, I don't know how much money you have free to invest in setting up a cleverly targeted promotion, or how much faith you have in it working, in Soul Shine's actual appeal to the people but I know this can work. I admit I f*cked up with aiming at snobby ass high ups but this is to the people, the actual audience of the music, the ones who'll actually feel the energy in it and be moved by it, share it with their friends and help it spread like wildfire."

Janika clicked on some of the other internet tabs that showed graphs and studies and success stories of people growing their youtube brand with promotion. "How much paper this going to cost?"

"Twenty bucks can reach a hundred k people."

"And what if I had a thousand saved up?"

"Millions would be exposed to Soul Shine's brilliance. All we need is a music video for one of their songs."

Janika rubbed Sales shoulder. "Sh*t, I've already got the perfect idea for that. Have for a long time. We film them in near complete darkness and whenever one is doing a verse or chorus, that one steps out of the dark into visible light and rocks their vocals before stepping back into the dark as the other steps out to go at it. It's like the music is saving them from the dark, the pain, like they're lost and then their music gives this powerful lyrical strength and magic, hope and light."

Sales nodded, thinking on it. "You know you're a genius right?"

Janika posed a little. "I know, I know, haha."

She grabbed her phone and got in contact with Soul Shine who seemed in better moods too with a new day and agreed to come over asap to shoot the music video. Janika suggested they use her building's basement as it would be perfect for capturing the 'in and out of darkness' effect they wanted. They found an area of the basement where a slit of light cut across from a street level, tiny window and set up to film using only Janika's phone camera. Soul shine arrived and hid their worry at the state of the basement with excitement to work and get somewhere. Jerone and Sales slapped hands and watched Cedrice and Janika who embraced in a hug. Cedrice held Janika tight. "My bad on my attitude yesterday, fam. Sh*t was.."

Janika kissed her head. "Don't even sweat it. I feel you and I got you, sister."

The dudes sighed relief and everyone got to hustling. Janika showed Soul Shine how she wanted them to be stepping in and out of the dark and light and where the exact line was it would be clear while Sales filmed them talking to get an idea of how close he would have to be with the phone while filming to get clear audio. Once all that was sorted, they stood close, nervous but excited to start getting takes done. Jerone took some deep breaths with eyes closed, centered himself to get his focus right while Cedrice spat a few random lyrics to warm her bars up. Sales put a hand on both of their shoulders and looked back and forth between their eyes with a look of his own that carried so many stories of pain yet survival, of fighting through hopeless to win, of being dragged down but rising up again and Soul Shine felt themselves lifted, felt a powerful flowing energy enter them. Sales gave them a nod and moved to his mark to record. Janika pressed play on the beat they chose on Cedrice's phone as Jerone sang harmony with it and on the mark of 4 beats, Cedrice stepped out of the darkness, into the light. "Ima step out of these shadows where ghosts be haunting us fam, all the bullshit of the past that's got us feeling cursed, damn. I never understand how we still be treated second class, I tell you right now that it won't be the end of us."

The beat steps up. "I tell you right now that we aren't no damn lesser beings, scars upon our history show survival of fittest. I remember daddy beaten by the shield just for walking streets, I remember mumma beaten in her home just for being cheek. What's a lil girl, lil boy meant to think, when we watch our people pushed to brink, pushed to brink. Time to send these folks a memo.. we are the kings and queens!"

The beat eased back and Cedrice stepped back into the darkness which was followed by Jerone stepping into the light. "Ohhhh, this world can be so cruel. Ohhh, lost boys n girls I see you. My brothers, my sisters, we can't let the blood spilled dictate us. Our futures, our pasts, there's one that's in the hands of us. And I knooooow that it don't feel like we got control. We gotta grooooow, use ambition to counter their blows."

Jerone stepped back into the dark and Cedrice stepped out again as the beat quickened. "See ima show the good ol boys the shine of a n****r heart, blind a mother*cker with the grind of a n****r heart. They can have their old school sh*t fam, but ima start a new wave kingdom, new wave queendom, sisters rise, brothers too, melanin sunrise. Ain't no pigeonholing on ourselves cause we know our truths, rolling with a deeper strength than any other race can do!"

Cedrice stepped back into the dark as the beat softened and slowed with Jerone's stepping out. "My mumma used to say that I was her little king, yet I couldn't see a throne so I built one from within. Build your throne my brothers and sisterssss. Grind your dream, we can't afford to be quitersssss. Ohhhhh I know it hurts, and I know it's hard. Them odds stacked high but we born to fly. If we give up nooowww, then the future diieess. Please don't give up noooowww. Let's unite and riiissseee."

They did another verse and chorus before the end of the song and both stepped out of the dark, sweating hard from the dank basement heat and performing with so much heart. They knew from seeing and hearing each other go at it that they could be proud of what they did but they also looked with nervous hope to Sales and Janika. Janika screamed "oh my god, you brilliant mother*ckers! You killed it! You god damn killed it!"

She embraced them both as Sales started watching the video to see if it recorded well enough and how the performance came across through being recorded. The others quickly rushed to see too and all watched the entire recorded performance. Janika started pacing in tight lines. "That's it! That's mother*cking it, yo! That's the one! Upload that right now and let me put a k on promoting it to all the brothers and sisters across our country!"

Soul Shine looked shocked, in a good way. Cedrice touched Janika's arm. "For real? You're going to put a grand on us? On that performance? To blow us up?"

"Hell yes! I'd put a 100 k on it if I had it, damn!"

Jerone hugged Janika. "Much love, sister. Thank you."

Cedrice watched Sales upload the video and set the promotion specifics. "I'm all out of words, fam. The appreciation is deep."

Sales finished entering all the details and handed Janika back her phone to enter the money and card details which she did with great enthusiasm and confirmed it all. "How long do you think it'll take before people start seeing it?"

Sales replied. "It can take up to 24 hours but views and comments can start coming through right away. It usually doesn't take long for youtube to approve the promotion."

Cedrice bit her lip. "I bet those mother*ckers won't allow it! I swear to god, if the system try n hold us down again.."

Sales interrupted. "Even if the promotion isn't approved, which I don't see why it wouldn't be, people will still be able to see the video, the song on youtube."

Cedrice nodded. "Cool, cool."

Janika said "let's go grab a feed or something to keep our minds off it a bit."

"Aight."

By the time they made it out to the street, a notification popped up on Janika's phone. She checked it and grinned. "Yo, fuckers, check it."

She held up her phone to show the song already had a handful of likes and a positive comment showing mad love for the song. "That's already, yo. Already! Shit ain't even been approved yet."

Jerone leant in closer, read out the comment. "Thank you so much, I really needed to hear this right now."

Sales actually smiled warmly. He could feel his purpose actually beginning to happen, the reason he dragged himself out of hell to this mortal world, to spark some greater change in how things are. As the day rolled on, more and more likes and comments of love piled up on the song and by the time night fell, the video, the song had gone viral and that was before youtube had even approved the promotion. The dream was happening for all of them, Soul Shine and Till the flames management. That song changed all their lives and affected to many more around their country and the world and it was only the beginning of their new journey.

THE END

(Please leave a review if you enjoyed this and feel free to email me and let me know which story was your favorite. You might also like to check out one of my other erotica collections 'LGBT lust and love')

www.ingramcontent.com/pod-product-compliance
Lightning Source LLC
Chambersburg PA
CBHW052124150726
48002CB00006B/2487